The Blunders of
a Bashful Man

Walter T. Gray

Blunders of a
Bashful Man

By the Author of A BAD BOY'S DIARY

J. S. OGILVIE PUBLISHING COMPANY

57 Rose Street, New York, N. Y.

THE BLUNDERS

OF A

BASHFUL MAN.

By the Author of

"A BAD BOY'S DIARY"

1881

CONTENTS

CHAPTER I.

HE ATTENDS A PICNIC.

I have been, am now, and shall always be, a bashful man. I have been told that I am the only bashful man in the world. How that is I can not say, but should not be sorry to believe that it is so, for I am of too generous a nature to desire any other mortal to suffer the mishaps which have come to me from this distressing complaint. A person can have smallpox, scarlet fever, and measles but once each. He can even become so inoculated with the poison of bees and mosquitoes as to make their stings harmless; and he can gradually accustom, himself to the use of arsenic until he can take 444 grains safely; but for bashfulness—like mine—there is no first and only attack, no becoming hardened to the thousand petty stings, no saturation of one's being with the poison until it loses its power.

I am a quiet, nice-enough, inoffensive young gentleman, now rapidly approaching my twenty-sixth year. It is unnecessary to state that I am unmarried. I should have been wedded a great many times, had not some fresh attack of my malady invariably, and in some new shape, attacked me in season to prevent the "consummation devoutly to be wished." When I look back over twenty years of suffering through which I have literally stumbled my way—over the long series of embarrassments and mortifications which lie behind me—I wonder, with a mild and patient wonder, why the Old Nick I did not commit suicide ages ago, and thus end the eventful history with a blank page in the middle of the book. I dare say the very bashfulness which has been my bane has prevented me; the idea of being cut down from a rafter, with a black-and-blue face, and drawn out of the water with a swollen one, has put me so out of countenance that I had not the courage to brave a coroner's jury under the circumstances.

Life to me has been a scramble through briers. I do not recall one single day wholly free from the scratches inflicted on a cruel sensitiveness. I will not mention those far-away agonies of boyhood, when the teacher punished me by making me sit with the girls, but will hasten on to a point that stands out vividly against a dark background of accidents. I was nineteen. My sentiments toward that part of creation known as "young ladies" were, at that time, of a mingled and contradictory nature. I adored them as angels; I dreaded them as if they were mad dogs, and were going to bite me.

My parents were respected residents of a small village in the western part of the State of New York. I had been away at a boys' academy for three years, and returned about the first of June to my parents and to Babbletown to find that I was considered a young man, and expected to take my part in the business and pleasures of life as such. My father dismissed his clerk and put me in his place behind the counter of our store.

Within three days every girl in that village had been to that store after something or another—pins, needles, a yard of tape, to look at gloves, to *try on shoes*, or examine gingham and calico, until I was happy, because out of sight, behind a pile high enough to hide my flushed countenance. I shall never forget that week. I ran the gauntlet from morning till night. I believe those heartless wretches told each other the mistakes I made, for they kept coming and coming, looking as sweet as honey and as sly as foxes. Father said I'd break him if I didn't stop making blunders in giving change—he wasn't in the prize-candy business, and couldn't afford to have me give twenty-five sheets of note paper, a box of pens, six corset laces, a bunch of whalebones, and two dollars and fifty cents change for a two-dollar bill.

He explained to me that the safety-pins which I had offered Emma Jones for crochet-needles were *not* crochet-needles; nor the red wafers I had shown Mary Smith for gum-drops, gum-drops—that gingham was not three dollars per yard, nor pale-blue silk twelve-and-a-half cents, even to Squire Marigold's daughter. He said I must be more careful.

"I don't think the mercantile business is my *forte*, father," said I.

2

"Your fort!" replied the old gentleman; "fiddlesticks! We have nothing to do with military matters. But if you think you have a special call to anything, John, speak out. Would you like to study for the ministry, my son?"

"Oh, no, indeed! I don't know exactly what I would like, unless it were to be a Juan Fernandez, or a—a light-house keeper."

Then father said I was a disgrace to him, and I knew I was.

On the fourth day some young fellows came to see me, and told me there was to be a picnic on Saturday, and I must get father's horse and buggy and take one of the girls. In vain I pleaded that I did not know any of them well enough. They laughed at me, and said that Belle Marigold had consented to go with me; that I knew her—she had been in the store and bought some blue silk for twelve-and-a-half cents a yard; and they rather thought she fancied me, she seemed so ready to accept my escort; should they tell her I would call for her at ten o'clock, sharp, on Saturday morning?

There was no refusing under the circumstances, and I said "yes" with the same gaiety with which I would have signed my own death-warrant. Yet I wanted to go to the picnic, dreadfully; and of all the young ladies in Babbletown I preferred Belle Marigold. She was the handsomest and most stylish girl in the county. Her eyes were large, black, and mischievous; her mouth like a rose; she dressed prettily, and had an elegant little way of tossing back her dark ringlets that was fascinating even at first sight. I was told my doom on Thursday afternoon, and do not think I slept any that or Friday night—am positive I did not Saturday night. I wanted to go and I wanted to take that particular girl, yet I was in a cold sweat at the idea. I would have given five dollars to be let off, and I wouldn't have taken fifteen for my chance to go. I asked father if I could have the horse and buggy, and if he would tend store. I hoped he would say No; but when he said Yes, I was delighted.

"I'll take the opportunity when you are at the picnic to get the accounts out of the quirks you've got 'em into," said he.

Well, Saturday came. As I opened my eyes my heart jumped into my throat. "I've got to go through with it now if it kills me," I thought.

Mother asked me why I ate no breakfast.

"Saving my appetite for the picnic," I responded, cheerfully; which was one of the white lies my miserable bashfulness made me tell every day of my life—I knew that I should go dinner-less at the picnic unless I could get behind a tree with my plate of goodies.

I never to this day can abide to eat before strangers; things *always* go by my windpipe instead of my æsophagus, and I'm tired to death of scalding my legs with hot tea, to say nothing of adding to one's embarrassment to have people asking if one has burned oneself, and feeling that one has broken a cup out of a lady's best china tea-set. But about tea and tea-parties I shall have more to say hereafter. I must hurry on to my first picnic, where I made my first public appearance as the Bashful Man.

I made a neat toilet—a fresh, light summer suit that I flattered myself beat any other set of clothes in Babbletown—ordered Joe, our chore-boy, to bring the buggy around in good order, with everything shining; and when he had done so, had the horse tied in front of the store.

"Come, my boy," said father, after a while, "it's ten minutes to ten. Never keep the ladies waiting."

"Yes, sir; as soon as I've put these raisins away."

"Five minutes to ten, John. Don't forget the lemons."

"No, sir." But I *did* forget them in my trepidation, and a man had to be sent back for them afterward.

It was just ten when I stepped into the buggy with an attempt to appear in high spirits. As I drove slowly toward Squire Marigold's large mansion on Main Street, I met dozens of gay young folks on the way out of town, some of them calling out that I would be late, and to try and catch up with them after I got my girl.

As I came in sight of the house my courage failed. I turned off on a by-street, drove around nearly half a mile, and finally approached the object of my dread from another direction. I do believe I should have passed the house after I got to it had I not seen a vision of pink ribbons, white dress, and black eyes at the window, and realized that I was observed. So I touched the horse with the whip, drove up with a flourish, and before I had fairly pulled up at the block, Belle was at the door, with a servant behind her carrying a hamper.

"You are late, Mr. Flutter," she called out, half gayly, half crossly.

I arose from the seat, flung down the reins, and leaped out, like a flying-fish out of the water, to hand the beautiful apparition in. In my nervousness I did not observe how I placed the lines, my foot became entangled in them, I was brought up in the most unexpected manner, landing on the pavement on my new hat instead of the soles of my boots.

This was not only embarrassing, but positively painful. There was a bump on my forehead, the rim of my hat was crushed, my new suit was soiled, my knee ached like Jericho, and there was a rent in my pantaloons right opposite where my knee hurt.

Belle tittered, the colored girl stuffed her apron in her mouth, and said "hi! hi!" behind it. I would have given all I had in life to give if I could have started on an exploring expedition for China just then, but I couldn't. The pavement was not constructed with reference to swallowing up bashful young men who wanted to be swallowed.

"I hope you are not hurt, Mr. Flutter, te-he?"

"Oh, not at all, not in the least; it never hurts me to fall. It was those constricted reins, they caught my foot. Does the basket go with us? I mean the servant. No, I don't, I mean the basket—does she go with us?"

"The hamper does, Mr. Flutter, or we should be minus sandwiches. Jane, put the hamper in."

Miss Marigold was in the buggy before I had straightened my hat-rim.

"I hope your horse is a fast one; we shall be late," she remarked, as I took my place by her side. "Here is a pin, Mr. Flutter; you can pin up that tear."

I was glad she asked me to let the horse go at full speed; it was the most soothing thing which could happen at that time. As he flew along I could affect to be busy with the cares of driving, and so escape the trials of conversation. I spoke to my lovely companion only three times in the eight miles between her house and the grove. The first time I remarked, "We are going to have a warm day"; the second, "I think the day will be quite warm"; the third time I launched out boldly: "Don't you think, Miss Marigold, we shall have it rather warm about noon?"

"You seem to feel the heat more than I do," she answered, demurely, which was true, for she looked as cool as a cucumber and as comfortable as a mouse in a cheese, while I was mopping my face every other minute with my handkerchief.

When we reached the picnic grounds she offered to hold the reins while I got out. As I lifted her down, the whole company, who had been watching for our arrival, burst out laughing. Miss Belle looked at me and burst out laughing, too.

"What's the matter?" I stammered.

"Oh, nothing," said she; "only you dusted your clothes with your handkerchief after you fell, and now you've wiped your face with it, and it's all streaked up as if you'd been making mud pies, and your hat's a little out of shape, and—"

"You look as if you'd been on a bender," added the fellow who had induced me to come to the confounded affair.

"Well, I guess I can wash my face," I retorted, a little mad. "I've met with an accident, that's all. Just wait until I've tied my horse."

There was a pond close by—part of the programme of the picnic was to go out rowing on the pond—and as soon as I had fastened my horse, I went down to the bank and stooped over to wash my face, and the bank gave way and I pitched headlong into twelve feet of water.

I was not scared, for I could swim, but I was puzzled as to how to enjoy a picnic in my wet clothes. I wanted to go home, but the boys said:

"No—I must walk about briskly and let my things dry on me—the day was so warm I wouldn't take cold."

So I walked about briskly, all by myself, for about two hours, while the rest of them were having a good time. Then some one asked where the lemons were that I was to bring, and I had to confess that they were at home in the store, and dinner was kept waiting another two hours while a man took my horse and went for those lemons. I walked about all the time he was gone, and was dry enough by the time the lemonade was made to wish I had some. But the water had shrunk my clothes so that the legs of my pantaloons and the arms of my coat were about six inches too short, while my boots, which had been rather tight in the first place, made my feet feel as if they were in a red-hot iron vise. I couldn't face all those giggling girls, and I got down behind a tree and the tears came in my eyes, I felt so miserable.

Belle was a tease, but she wasn't heartless; she got two plates, heaped with nice things, and two tumblers of lemonade, and sat down by my side coaxing me to eat, and telling me how sorry she was that I had had my pleasure destroyed by an accident.

I had a piece of spring chicken, but being too bashful to masticate it properly, I attempted to swallow it whole. It stuck!—she had to pat me on the back—I became purple and kicked about wildly, ruining her new sash by upsetting both plates. She became seriously alarmed, and ran for aid; two of the fellows stood me on my head and pounded the soles of my feet, by which wise course the morsel was dislodged, and "Richard was himself again."

After the excitement had partially subsided, the punster of the village—there is always one punster in every community—broke out with:

"Oh, swallow, swallow, flying South, fly to her and tell her what I tell to thee."

The girls laughed; I looked and saw Belle trying to wipe the ice-cream from her sash.

"Never mind the sash, Miss Marigold," I said, in desperation, "I'll send you another to-morrow. But if you'll excuse me, I'll go home now. I'm not well, and mother'll be alarmed about me—I ought not to have left father alone to tend store, and I feel that I've taken cold. I presume some of these folks will have a spare seat, and my boots have shrunk, and I don't care for picnics as a general thing, anyway. My clothes are shrinking all the time, and I think we're going to have a thunder-shower, and I guess I'll go."—and I went.

CHAPTER II.

HE MAKES AN EVENING CALL.

It's very provoking to a bashful man to have the family pew only one remove from the pulpit. I didn't feel like going to church the day after the picnic, but father wouldn't let me off. I caught my foot in a hole in the carpet walking up the aisle, which drew particular attention to me; and dropped by hymn-book twice, to add to the interest I had already excited in the congregation. My fingers are always all thumbs when I have to find the hymn.

"I do believe you did take cold yesterday," said mother, when we came out. "You must have a fever, for your face is as red as fire."

Very consoling when a young man wants to look real sweet. But that's my luck. I'll be as pale as a poet when I leave my looking-glass, but before I enter a ball-room or a dining-room I'll be as red as an alderman. I have often wished that I could be permanently whitewashed, like a kitchen wall or a politician's record. I think, perhaps, if I were whitewashed for a month or two I might cure myself of my habit of blushing when I enter a room. I bought a box of "Meen Fun" once, and tried to powder; but I guess I didn't understand the art as well as the women do; it was mean fun in good earnest, for the girl I was going to take to singing-school wanted to know if I'd been helping my ma make biscuits for supper; and then she took her handkerchief and brushed my face, which wasn't so bad as it might have been, for her handkerchief had patchouly on it and was as soft as silk. But that wasn't Belle Marigold, and so it didn't matter.

To return to church. I went again in the evening, and felt more at home, for the kerosene was not very bright. I got along without any accident. After meeting was out, father stopped to speak to the minister. As I stood in the entry, waiting for him, Belle came out, and asked me how I felt after the picnic. I saw she was alone, and so I hemmed, and said: "Have you any one to see you home?"

She said, "No; but I'm not afraid—it's not far," and stopped and waited for me to offer her my arm, looking up at me with those bewitching eyes.

"Oh," said I, dying to wait upon her, but not daring to crook my elbow before the crowd, "I'm glad of that; but if you are the least bit timid, Miss Marigold, father and I will walk home with you."

Then I heard a suppressed laugh behind me, and, turning, saw that detestable Fred Hencoop, who never knew what it was to feel modest since the day his nurse tied his first bib on him.

"Miss Marigold," said he, looking as innocent as a lamb, "if you do me the honor to accept my arm, I'll try and take you home without calling on my pa to assist me in the arduous duty." And she went with him.

I was very low-spirited on the way home.

"As sure as I live I'll go and call on her to-morrow evening, and show her I'm not the fool she thinks I am," I said, between my gritted teeth. "I'll take her a new sash to replace the one I spoiled at the picnic, and we'll see who's the best fellow, Hencoop or I."

The next afternoon I measured off four yards of the sweetest sash-ribbon ever seen in Babbletown, and charged myself with seven dollars—half my month's salary, as agreed upon between father and me—and rolled up the ribbon in white tissue paper, preparatory to the event of the evening.

"Where are you going?" father asked, as I edged out of the store just after dark.

"Oh, up the street a piece."

"Well, here's a pair o' stockings to be left at the Widow Jones'. Just call as you go by and leave 'em, will you?"

I stuck the little bundle he gave me in my coat-tail pocket; but by the time I passed the Widow Jones' house I was so taken up with the business on hand that I forgot all about the stockings.

I could see Miss Marigold sitting at the piano and hear her singing as I passed the window. It was awful nice, and, to prolong the pleasure, I stayed outside about half an hour, then a summer shower came up, and I made up my mind and rang the bell. Jane came to the door.

"Is the squire at home?" says I.

"No, sir, he's down to the hotel; but Miss Marigold, she's to hum," said the black girl, grinning. "Won't you step in? Miss will be dreffle sorry her pa is out."

She took my hat and opened the parlor door; there was a general dazzle, and I bowed to somebody and sat down somewhere, and in about two minutes the mist cleared away, and I saw Belle Marigold, with a rose in her hair, sitting not three feet away, and smiling at me as if coaxing me to say something.

"Quite a shower?" I remarked.

"Indeed—is it raining?" said she.

"Yes, indeed," said I; "it came up very sudden."

"I hope you didn't get wet?" said she, with a sly look.

"Not this time," said I, trying to laugh.

"Does it lighten?" said she.

"A few," said I.

Miss Marigold coughed and looked out of the window. There was a pause in our brilliant conversation.

"I think we shall have a rainy night," I resumed.

"I'm *so* afraid of thunder," said she. "I shall not sleep a bit if it thunders. I shall sit up until the rain is over. I never like to be alone in a storm. I always want some one *close by me*," she said, with a little shiver.

"I'M SO FRIGHTENED, MR. FLUTTER," SAID SHE; "I FEEL, IN
MOMENTS LIKE THESE, HOW SWEET IT WOULD BE TO HAVE
SOME ONE TO CLING TO."

I hitched my chair about a foot nearer hers. It thundered pretty loud,
and she gave a little squeal, and brought her chair alongside mine.

"I'm so frightened, Mr. Flutter," said she: "I feel, in moments like
these, how sweet it would be to have someone to cling to."

And she glanced at me out of the corner of her eye.

"Dear Belle," said I, "would you—would you—could you—now—"

"What?" whispered she, very softly.

"If I thought," I stammered, "that you could—that you would—that
it was handy to give me a drink of water." She sprang up as if shot,
and rang a little hand-bell.

"Jane, a glass of water for this gentleman—*ice*-water," in a very chilly
tone, and she sat down over by the piano.

Bashful fool and idiot that I was. I had lost another opportunity.

After I had swallowed the water Jane had left the room. I bethought
me of the handsome present which I had in my pocket, and, hoping

to regain her favor by that, I drew out the little package and tossed it carelessly in her lap.

"Belle," said I, "I have not forgotten that I spilled lemonade on your sash; I hope you will not refuse to allow me to make such amends as are in my power. If the color does not suit you, I will exchange it for any you may select."

She began to smile again, coquettishly untying the string and unwrapping the paper. Instead of the lovely rose-colored ribbon, out rolled a long pair of coarse blue cotton stockings.

Miss Marigold screamed louder than she had at the thunder.

"It's all a mistake!" I cried; "a ridiculous mistake! I beg your pardon ten thousand times! They are for the Widow Jones. *Here* is what I intended for *you*, dear, dear Belle," and I thrust another package into heir hands.

"Fine-cut!" said she, examining the wrapper by the light of the lamp on the piano. "Do you think I chew, Mr. Flutter?—or *dip*? Do you intend to willfully insult me? Leave the hou——"

"Oh, I beg of you, listen! Here it is at last!" I exclaimed in desperation, drawing out the right package at last, and myself displaying to her dazzled view the four yards of glittering ribbon. "There's not another in Babbletown so handsome. Wear it for *my sake*, Belle!"

"I will," she sighed, after she had secretly rubbed it, and held it to the light to make sure of its quality. "I will, John, for your sake."

We were friends again; she was very sweet, and played something on the piano, and an hour slipped away as if I were in Paradise. I rose to go, the rain being over.

"But about that paper of fine-cut!" she said, archly, as she went into the hall with me to get my hat; "do you chew, John?"

"No, Belle, that tobacco was for old man Perkins, as sure as I stand here. If you don't believe me, smell my breath," said I, and I tried to get my arm about her waist.

It was kind of dark in the hall; she did not resist so very much; my lips were only about two inches from hers—for I wanted her to be sure about my breath—when a voice that almost made me faint away, put a conundrum to me:

"If you'd a kissed my girl, young man, why would it have been like a Centennial fire-arm?"

"Because it hasn't gone off yet!" I gasped, reaching for my hat.

"Wrong," said he grimly. "Because it would have been a blunder-buss."

I reckon the squire was right.

CHAPTER III.

GOES TO A TEA-PARTY.

The Widow Jones got her stockings the next day. As I left them at the door she stuck her head out of an upper window and said to me that "the sewing society met at her house on Thursday afternoon, and the men-folks was coming to tea and to spend the evening, and I must be *sure* an' come, or the girls would be *so* disappointed," and she urged and urged until I had to promise her I would attend her sociable.

Drat all tea-parties! say I. I was never comfortable at one in my life. If you'd give me my choice between going to a tea-party and picking potato-bugs off the vines all alone on a hot summer day, I shouldn't hesitate a moment between the two. I should choose the bugs; and I can't say I fancy potato-bugs, either.

On Wednesday I nearly killed an old lady, putting up tartar-emetic for cream-tartar. If she'd eaten another biscuit made with it she'd have died and I'd have been responsible—and father was really vexed and said I might be a light-house keeper as quick as I pleased; but by that time I felt as if I couldn't keep a light-house without Belle Marigold to help me, and so I promised to be more careful, and kept on clerking.

The thermometer stood at eighty degrees in the shade when I left the store at five o'clock Thursday afternoon to go to that infallible tea-party. I was glad the day was warm, for I wanted to wear my white linen suit, with a blue cravat and Panama hat. I felt independent even of Fred Hencoop, as I walked along the street under the shade of the elms; but, the minute I was inside Widow Jones' gate and walking up to the door, the thermometer went up to somewhere near 200 degrees. There were something like a dozen heads at each of the parlor windows, and all women's heads at that. Six or eight more were peeping out of the sitting-room, where they were laying the table for tea. Babbletown always did seem to me to have more than its fair share of female population. I think I would like to live in one of those mining towns out in Colorado, where women are as scarce as hairs on the inside of a man's hand. Somebody coughed as I was going up the walk. Did you ever have a girl cough at you?—one of those mean, teasing, expressive little coughs?

I had practiced—at home in my own room—taking off my Panama with a graceful, sweeping bow, and saying in calm, well-bred tones: "Good-evening, Mrs. Jones. Good-evening, ladies. I trust you have had a pleasant as well as profitable afternoon."

I had *practiced* that in the privacy of my chamber. What I really did get off was something like this:

"Good Jones, Mrs. Evening. I should say, good-evening, widows— ladies, I beg your pardon," by which time I was mopping my forehead with my handkerchief, and could just ask, as I sank into the first chair I saw, "Is your mother well, Mrs. Jones?" which was highly opportune, since said mother had been years dead before I was born. As I sat down, a pang sharper than some of those endured by the Spartans ran through my right leg. I was instantly aware that I had plumped down on a needle, as well as a piece of fancy-work, but I had not the courage to rise and extract the excruciating thing.

I turned pale with pain, but by keeping absolutely still I found that I could endure it, and so I sat motionless, like a wooden man, with a frozen smile on my features.

Belle was out in the other room helping set the table, for which mitigating circumstances I was sufficiently thankful.

Fred Hencoop was on the other side of the room holding a skein of silk for Sallie Brown. He looked across at me, smiling with a malice which made me hate him.

Out of that hate was born a stern resolve—I would conquer my diffidence; I would prove to Fred Hencoop, and any other fellow like him, that I was as good as he was, and could at least equal him in the attractions of my sex.

There was a pretty girl sitting quite near me. I had been introduced to her at the picnic. It seemed to me that she was eyeing me curiously, but I was mad enough at Fred to show him that I could be as cool as anybody, after I got used to it. I hemmed, wiped the perspiration from my face—caused now more by the needle than by the heat—and remarked, sitting stiff as a ramrod and smiling like an angel:

"June is my favorite month, Miss Smith—is it yours? When I think of June I always think of strawberries and cream and ro-oh-oh-ses!"

It was the needle. I had forgotten in the excitement of the subject and had moved.

"*Is* anything the matter?" Miss Smith tenderly inquired.

"Nothing in the world, Miss Smith. I had a stitch in my side, but it is over now."

"Stitches are very painful," she observed, sympathizingly. "I don't like to trouble you, Mr. Flutter, but I think, I believe, I guess you are sitting on my work. If you will rise, I will try and finish it before tea."

No help for it, and I arose, at the same moment dexterously slipping my hand behind me and withdrawing the thorn in the flesh.

"Oh, dear, where is my needle?" said the young lady, anxiously scrutinizing the crushed worsted-work.

I gave it to her with a blush. She burst out laughing.

"I don't wonder you had a stitch in your side," she remarked, shyly.

"Hem!" observed Fred very loud, "do you feel sew-sew, John?"

Just then Belle entered the parlor, looking as sweet as a pink, and wearing the sash I had given her. She bowed to me very coquettishly and announced tea.

"Too bad!" continued Fred; "you have broken the thread of Mr. Flutter's discourse with Miss Smith. But I do not wish to inflict *needle*-less pain, so I will not betray him."

"I hope Mr. Flutter is not in trouble again," said Belle quickly.

"Oh, no. Fred is only trying to say something *sharp*," said I.

"Come with me; I will take care of you, Mr. Flutter," said Belle, taking my arm and marching me out into the sitting-room, where a long table was heaped full of inviting eatables. She sat me down by her side, and I felt comparatively safe. But Fred and Miss Smith were just opposite and they disconcerted me.

"Mr. Flutter," said the hostess when it came my turn, "will you have tea or coffee?"

"Yes'm," said I.

"Tea or coffee?"

"If you please," said I.

"*Which*?" whispered Belle.

"Oh, excuse me; coffee, ma'am."

"Cream and sugar, Mr. Flutter?"

"I'm not particular which, Mrs. Jones."

"Do you take *both*?" she persisted, with everybody at the table looking my way.

"No, ma'am, only coffee," said I, my face the color of the beet-pickles.

She finally passed me a cup, and, in my embarrassment, I immediately took a swallow and burnt my mouth.

"Have you lost any friends lately?" asked that wretched Fred, seeing the tears in my eyes.

I enjoyed that tea-party as geese enjoy *pate de fois gras*. It was a prolonged torment under the guise of pleasure. I refused everything I wanted, and took everything I didn't want. I got a back of the cold chicken; there was nothing of it but bone. I thought I must appear to be eating it, and it slipped out from under my fork and flew into the dish of preserved cherries.

We had strawberries. I am very partial to strawberries and cream. I got a saucer of the berries, and was looking about for the cream when Miss Smith's mother, at my right hand, said:

"Mr. Flutter, will you have some *whip* with your strawberries?"

Whip with my berries! I thought she was making fun of me, and stammered:

"No, I thank you," and so I lost the delicious frothed cream that I coveted.

The agony of the thing was drawing to a close. I was longing for the time when I could go home and get some cold potatoes out of mother's cupboard. I hadn't eaten worth a cent.

Pretty soon we all moved back our chairs and rose. I offered my arm to Belle, as I supposed. Between the sitting-room and parlor there was a little dark hall, and when we got in there I summoned up courage, passed my arm around my fair partner, and gave her a hug.

"You ain't so bashful as you look," said she, and then we stepped into the parlor, and I found I'd been squeezing Widow Jones' waist.

She gave me a look full of languishing sweetness that scared me nearly to death. I thought of Mr. Pickwick and Mrs. Bardell. Visions of suits for breaches of promise arose before my horrified vision. I glanced wildly around in search of Belle; she was hanging on a young lawyer's arm, and not looking at me.

"La, now, you needn't color up so," said the widow, coquettishly, "I know what young men are."

She said it aloud, on purpose for Belle to hear. I felt like killing her. I might have done it, but one thought restrained me—I should be hung for murder, and I was too bashful to submit to so public an ordeal.

I hurried across the room to get rid of her. There was a young fellow standing there who looked about as out-of-place as I felt. I thought I would speak to him.

"Come," said I, "let us take a little promenade outside—the women are too much for me."

He made no answer. I heard giggling and tittering breaking out all around the room, like rash on a baby with the measles.

"Come on," said I; "like as not they're laughing at us."

"Look-a-here, you shouldn't speak to a fellow till you've been introduced," said that wicked Fred behind me. "Mr. Flutter, allow me to make you acquainted with Mr. Flutter. He's anxious to take a little walk with you."

It was so; I had been talking to myself in a four-foot looking-glass.

I did not feel like staying for the ice-cream and kissing-plays, but had a sly hunt for my hat, and took leave of the tea-party about the eighth of a second afterward.

CHAPTER IV.

HE DOES HIS DUTY AS A CITIZEN.

Babbletown began to be very lively as soon as the weather got cool, the fall after I came home. We had a singing-school once a week, a debating society that met every Wednesday evening, and then we had sociables, and just before Christmas a fair. All the other young men had a good time. Every day, when some of them dropped in the store for a chat and a handful of raisins, they would aggravate me by asking:

"*Aren't* we having a jolly winter of it, John?"

I never had a good time. *I* never enjoyed myself like other folks. I spent enough money and made enough good resolutions, but something always occurred to destroy my anticipated pleasure. I can't hear a lyceum or debating society mentioned to this day, without feeling "cold-chills" run down my spine.

I took part in the exercises the evening ours was opened. I had been requested by the committee to furnish the poem for the occasion. As I was just from a first-class academy, where I had read the valedictory, it was taken for granted that I was the most likely one to "fill the bill."

I accepted the proposition. To be bashful is a far different thing from being modest. I wrote the poem. I sat up nights to do it. The way candles were consumed caused father to wonder where his best box of spermacetis had gone to. I knew I could do the poetry, and I firmly resolved that I would read it through, from beginning to end, in a clear, well-modulated voice, that could be heard by all, including the minister and Belle Marigold. I would not blush, or stammer, or get a frog in my throat. I swore solemnly to myself that I would not. *Some folks* should see that my bashfulness was wearing off faster than the gold from an oroide watch. Oh, I would show 'em! Some things could be done as well as others. I would no longer be the laughing-stock of Babbletown. My past record should be wiped out! I would write my poem, and I would *read it* — read it calmly and impressively, so as to do full justice to it.

I got the poem ready. I committed it to memory, so that if the lights were dim, or I lost my place, I should not be at the mercy of the manuscript. The night came. I entered the hall with Belle on my arm, early, so as to secure her a front seat.

"Keep cool, John," were her whispered words, as I left her to take my place on the platform.

"Oh, I shall be cool enough. I know every line by heart; have said it to myself one hundred and nineteen times without missing a word."

I'm not going to bore you with the poem here; but will give the first four lines as they were *written* and as I *spoke* them:

> "Hail! Babbletown, fair village of the plain!
> Hail! friends and fellow-citizens. In vain
> I strive to sing the glories of this place,
> Whose history back to early times I trace."

The room was crowded, the president of the society made a few opening remarks, which closed by presenting Mr. Flutter, the poet of the occasion. I was quite easy and at home until I arose and bowed as he spoke my name. Then something happened to my senses, I don't know what; I only knew I lost every one of them for about two minutes. I was blind, deaf, dumb, tasteless, senseless, and feelingless. Then I came to a little, rallied, and perceived that some of the boy were beginning to pound the floor with their heels. I made a feint of holding my roll of verses nearer the lamp at my right hand, summoned traitor memory to return, and began:

"Hail!"

Was that my voice? I did not recognize it. It was more as if a mouse in the gallery had squeaked. It would never do. I cleared any throat — which was to have been free from frogs — and a strange, hoarse voice, no more like mine than a crow is like a nightingale, came out with a jerk, about six feet away, and remarked, as if surprised:

"Hail!"

With a desperate effort, I resolved that this night or never I was to achieve greatness. I cleared the way again and recommenced:

"Hail!"

A boy's voice at the back of the room was heard to insinuate that perhaps it would be easier for me to let it snow or rain. That made me angry. I was as cool as ice all in a moment; I felt that I had the mastery of the situation, and, making a sweeping gesture with my left hand, I looked over my hearers' heads, and continued:

"Hail! Fabbletown, bare village of the plain—Babbletown, fair pillage of the vain—. Hail! friends and fellow-citizens—!"

It was evident that I had borrowed somebody else's voice—my own mother wouldn't have recognized it—and a mighty poor show of a voice, too. It was like a race-horse that suddenly balks, and loses the race. I had put up heavy stakes on that voice, but I couldn't budge it. Not an inch faster would it go. In vain I whipped and spurred in silent desperation—it balked at "fellow-citizens," and there it stuck. The audience, good-naturedly, waited five minutes. At the end of that time, I sat down, amid general applause, conscious that I had made the sensation of the evening.

Belle gave me the mitten that evening, and went home in Fred Hencoop's sleigh.

We didn't speak, after that, until about a week before the fair. She, with some other girls, then came in the store to beg for "scraps" of silk, muslin, and so-forth, to dress dolls for the fair. They were very sweet, for they knew they could make a fool of me. Father was not in, and I guess they timed their visit so that he wouldn't be. They got half a yard of pink silk, as much of blue, ditto of lilac and black, a yard of every kind of narrow ribbon in the store, a remnant of book-muslin, three yards—in all, about six dollars' worth of "scraps," and then asked me if I wasn't going to give a box of raisins and the coffee for the table. I said I would.

"And you'll come, Mr. Flutter, won't you? It'll be a failure unless *you* are there. You must *promise* to come. We won't go out of this store till you do. And, oh, don't forget to bring *your purse* along. We expect all the young gentlemen to *come prepared*, you know."

There is no doubt that I went to the fair. It made my heart ache to do it—for I'd already been pretty extravagant, one way and another—but I put a ten-dollar bill in my wallet, resolved to spend every cent of it rather than appear mean.

I don't know whether I appeared mean or not; I do know that I spent every penny of that ten dollars, and considerable more besides. If there was anything at that fair that no one else wanted, and that was not calculated to supply any known want of the human race, it was palmed off on me. I became the unhappy possessor of five dressed dolls, a lady's "nubia," a baby-jumper, fourteen "tidies," a set of parlor croquet with wickets that wouldn't stand on their legs, a patent churn warranted to make a pound of fresh butter in three minutes out of a quart of chalk-and-water, a set of ladies' nightcaps, two child's aprons, a castle-in-the-air, a fairy-palace, a doll's play-house, a toy-balloon, a box of marbles, a pair of spectacles, a pair of pillow-shams, a young lady's work-basket, seven needle-books, a cradle-quilt, a good many bookmarks, a sofa-cushion, and an infant's rattle, warranted to cut one's eye teeth; besides which I had tickets in a fruit cake, a locket, a dressing-bureau, a baby-carriage, a lady's watch-chain, and an infant's wardrobe complete.

When I feebly remonstrated that I'd spent all the money I brought, I was smilingly assured by innumerable female Tootses that "it was of no consequence"; but I found there *were* consequences when I came to settle afterward for half the things at the fair, because I was too bashful to say No, boldly.

Fred Hencoop auctioned off the remaining articles after eleven o'clock. Every time he put up something utterly unsalable, he would look over at me, nod, and say: "Thank you, John; did you say fifty cents?" or "Did I hear you say a dollar? A dollar—dollar—going, gone to our friend and patron, John Flutter, Jr.," and some of the lady managers would "make a note of it," and I was too everlastingly embarrassed to deny it.

"John," said father, about four o'clock in the afternoon the day after the fair—"John, did you buy all these things?"—the front part of the store was piled and crammed with my unwilling purchases.

"Father, I don't know whether I did or not."

"How much is the bill?"

"$98.17."

"How are you going to pay it?"

"I've got the hundred dollars in bank grandmother gave me when she died."

"Draw the money, pay your debts, and either get married at once and make these things useful, or we'll have a bonfire in the back yard."

"I guess we'd better have the bonfire, father. I don't care for any girl but Belle, and she won't have me."

"Won't have you! I'm worth as much as Squire Marigold any day."

"I know it, father; but I took her down to supper last night, and I was so confused, with all the married ladies looking on, I made a mess of it. I put two teaspoonfuls of sugar in her oyster stew, salted her coffee, and insisted on her taking pickles with her ice-cream. She didn't mind that so much, but when I stuffed my saucer into my pocket, and conducted her into the coal-cellar instead of the hall, she got out of patience. Father, I think I'd better go to Arizona in the spring. I'm—"

"Go to grass! if you want to," was the unfeeling reply; "but don't you ever go to another fair, unless I go along to take care of you."

But I think the bonfire made him feel better.

CHAPTER V.

HE COMMITS SUICIDE.

Two days after the fair (one day after the bonfire), some time during the afternoon, I found myself alone in the store. Business was so dull that father, with a yawn, said he guessed he'd go to the post-office and have a chat with the men.

"Be sure you don't leave the store a moment alone, John," was his parting admonition.

Of course I wouldn't think of such a thing—he need not have mentioned it. I was a good business fellow for my age; the only blunders I ever made were those caused by my failing—the unhappy failing to which I have hitherto alluded.

I sat mournfully on the counter after father left me, my head reclining pensively against a pile of ten-cent calicoes; I was thinking of my grandmother's legacy gone up in smoke—of how Belle looked when she found I had conducted her into the coal-cellar—of those tidies, cradle-quilts, bib-aprons, dolls' and ladies' fixings, which had been nefariously foisted upon me, a base advantage taken of my diffidence!—and I felt sad. I felt more than melancholy—I felt mad. I resented the tricks of the fair ones. And I made a mighty resolution! "Never—never—never," said I, between my clenched teeth, "will I again be guilty of the crime of bashfulness—*never!*"

I felt that I could face a female regiment—all Babbletown! I was indignant; and there's nothing like honest, genuine indignation to give courage. Oh, I'd show 'em. I wouldn't give a cent when the deacon passed the plate on Sundays; I wouldn't subscribe to the char——

In the midst of my dark and vengeful resolutions I heard merry voices on the pavement outside.

Hastily raising my head from the pile of calicoes, I saw at least five girls making for the store door—a whole bevy of them coming in upon me at once. They were the same rosy-cheeked, bright-eyed, deceitful, shameless creatures who had persuaded me into such folly at the fair. There was Hetty Slocum, the girl who coaxed me into buying the doll; and Maggie Markham, who sold me the quilt; and Belle, and two others, and they were chatting and giggling over some joke, and had to stop on the steps until they could straighten their faces. I grew fire-red—with indignation.

"Oh, father, why are you not here?" I cried inwardly. "Oh, father, what a shame to go off to the post-office and leave your son to face these tried to feel as I felt five minutes before, like facing a female regiment. *Now* was the time to prove my courage—to turn over a new leaf, take a new departure, begin life over again, show to these giggling girls that I had some pride—some self-independence—some self-resp——"

The door creaked on its hinges, and at the sound a blind confusion seized me. In vain I attempted, like a brave but despairing general, to rally my forces; but they all deserted me at once; I was hidden behind the calicoes, and with no time to arrange for a nobler plan of escaping a meeting with the enemy—no auger-hole though which to crawl. I followed the first impulse, stooped, and *hid under the counter.*

In a minute I wished myself out of that; but the minute had been too much—the bevy had entered and approached the counter, at the very place behind which I lay concealed. I was so afraid to breathe; the cold sweat started on my forehead.

"Why! there's no one in the store!" exclaimed Belle's voice.

"Oh, yes; there must be. Let us look around and see," responded Maggie, and they went tiptoeing around the room, peeping here and there, while I silently tore my hair. I was so afraid they would come behind the counter and discover me.

In three minutes, which seemed as many hours, they came to the starting-point again.

"There isn't a soul here."

"La, how funny! We might take something."

"Yes, if we were thieves, what a fine opportunity we would have."

"I'll bet three cents it's John's fault; his father would never leave the store in this careless way."

"What a queer fellow he is, anyway!"

"Ha, ha, ha! so perfectly absurd! *Isn't* it fun when he's about?"

"I never was so tickled in my life as when he bought that quilt."

"I thought I would die laughing when he took me into the coal-cellar, but I kept a straight face."

"Do *you* think he's good-looking, Hetty?"

"Who? John Flutter! *good-looking*? He's a perfect fright."

"That's just what I think. Oh, isn't it too good to see the way he nurses that little mustache of his? I'm going to send him a magnifying-glass, so that he can count the hairs with less trouble."

"If you will, I'll send a box of cold cream; we can send them through the post-office, and he'll never find out who they came from."

"Jolly! we'll do it! Belle won't send anything, for he's dead in love with *her*."

"Much good it'll do him, girls! Do you suppose I wouldn't marry that simpleton if he was made of gold."

"Did you ever see such a red face as he has? I would be afraid to come near it with a light dress on."

"And his ears!"

"Monstrous! and always burning."

"And the awkwardest fellow that ever blundered into a parlor. You know the night he waited on me to Hetty's party? he stepped on my toes so that I had to poultice them before I went to bed; he tore the train all off my pink tarlatan; he spilled a cup of hot coffee down old

Mrs. Ballister's back, and upset his saucer of ice-cream over Ada's sweet new book-muslin. Why, girls, just as sure as I am standing here, I saw him cram the saucer into his pocket when Belle came up to speak with him! I tell you, I was glad to get home that night without any more accidents."

"They say he always puts the tea-napkins into his pocket when he takes tea away from home. But it's not kleptomania, it's only bashfulness. I never heard before of his pocketing the saucers."

"Well, he really did. It's awful funny. I don't know how we'd get along without John this winter—he makes all the fun we have. What's that?"

"I don't know, it sounded like rats gnawing the floor."

(It was only the amusing John gritting his teeth, I am able to explain).

"Did you ever notice his mouth?—how large it is."

"Yes, it's frightful. I don't wonder he's ashamed of himself with that mouth."

"I don't mind his mouth so much—but his *nose*! I never did like a turn-up nose in a man. But his father's pretty well off. It would be nice to marry a whole store full of dry-goods and have a new dress every time you wanted one. I wonder where they have gone to! I believe I'll rap."

The last speaker seized the yard-stick and thumped on the counter directly over my head.

"Oh, girls! let's go behind, and see how they keep things. I wonder how many pieces of dress-silk there are left!"

"I guess I'll go behind the counter, and play clerk. If any one comes in, I'll go, as sure as the world! and wait on 'em. Won't it be fun? There comes old Aunty Harkness now. I dare say she is after a spool of thread or a paper of needles. I'm going to wait on her. Mr. Flutter won't care—I'll explain when he comes in. What do you want, auntie?" in a very loud voice.

My head buzzed like a saw—my heart made such a loud thud against my side I thought stars! she wanted "an ounce o' snuff," and that article was kept in a glass jar in plain sight on the other side of the store. There was a movement in that direction, and I recovered partially, I half resolved to rise up suddenly—pretend I'd been hiding for fun—and laugh the whole thing off as a joke. But the insulting, the ridiculous comments I had overheard, had made me too indignant. Pretty joke, indeed! But I wished I had obeyed the dictates of prudence and affected to consider it so. Father came bustling in while the girls were trying to tie up the snuff, and sneezing beautifully.

"What! what! young ladies! Where's John?"

"That's more than we know—tschi-he! We've been waiting at least ten minutes. Auntie Harkness wanted some stch-uff, and we thought we'd do it for her. I s'pose you've no objections, Mr. Flutter?"

"Not the least in the world, girls. Go ahead. I wonder where John is! There! you'll sneeze your pretty noses off—let me finish it. John has no business to leave the store. I don't like it—five cents, auntie, to *you*—and I told him particularly not to leave it a minute. I don't understand it; very sorry you've been kept waiting. What shall I show you, young lady?" and father passed behind the counter and stood with his toes touching my legs, notwithstanding I had shrunk into as small space as was convenient, considering my size and weight. It was getting toward dusk of the short winter afternoon, and I hoped and prayed he wouldn't notice me.

"What shall I show you, young ladies?"

"Some light kid gloves, No. 6, please."

"Yes, certainly—here they are. I do believe there's a strange dog under the counter! Get out—get out, sir, I say!" and my cruel parent gave me a vicious kick.

I pinched his leg impressively. I meant it as a warning, to betray to him that it was I, and to implore him, figuratively, to keep silence.

But he refused to comprehend that agonized pinch; he resented it. He gave another vicious kick. Then he stooped and looked under — it was a little dark — too dark, alas! under there. He saw a man — but not to recognize him.

"Ho!" he yelled; "robber! thief! burglar! I've got you, fellow! Come out o' that!"

I never before realized father's strength. He got his hand in my collar, and he jerked me out from under that counter, and shook me, and held me off at arm's length.

"There, Mr. Burglar," said he, triumphantly, "sneak in here again will — JOHN!"

The girls had been screaming and running, but they stood still now.

"Yes, *John!*" said I, in desperation. "The drawer came loose under the counter, and I was nailing on a strip of board when those *young ladies* came in. I kept quiet, just for fun. They began to talk in an interesting manner, curiosity got the better of politeness, and I'm afraid I've played eavesdropper," and I made a killing bow, meant especially for Belle.

"Well, you're a pretty one!" exclaimed father.

"*So they say,*" said I. "Don't leave, young ladies. I'd like to sell you a magnifying-glass, and some cold cream." But they all left in a hurry. They didn't even buy a pair of gloves.

The girls must have told of it, for the story got out, and Fred advised me to try counter-irritation for my bashfulness.

"You're not a burglar," said he, "but you're guilty of counter-fitting."

"Nothing would suit me better," I retorted, "than to be tried for it, and punished by solitary confinement."

And there was nothing I should have liked so much. The iron had entered my soul. I was worse than ever. I purchased a four-ounce vial of laudanum, went to my room, and wrote a letter to my mother:

"Mother, I am tired of life. My nose is turn-up, my mouth is large; I pocket other people's saucers and napkins; I am always making blunders. This is my last blunder. I shall never blush again. Farewell. Let the inscription on my tombstone be—'Died of Bashfulness.' JOHN."

And I swallowed the contents of the vial, and threw myself on my little bed.

CHAPTER VI.

HE IS DOOMED FOR WORSE ACCIDENTS.

It may seem strange for you to hear of me again, after the conclusion of the last chapter of my blunders. But it was not I who made the last blunder—it was the druggist. Quite by mistake the imbecile who waited upon me put up four ounces of the aromatic syrup of rhubarb. I felt myself gradually sinking into the death-sleep after I had taken it; with the thought of Belle uppermost in my mind, I allowed myself to sink—"no more catastrophes after this last and grandest one—no more red faces—big mouth—tea-napkins—wonder—if she—will be—sorry!" and I became unconscious.

I was awakened from a comfortable slumber by loud screams; mother stood by my bed, with the vial labeled "laudanum" in one hand, my letter in the other. Father rushed into the room.

"Father, John's committed suicide. Oh! bring the tartar-emetic quick! Make some coffee as strong as lye! Oh! send for a stomach-pump. Tell Mary to bring the things and put the coffee on; and you come here, an' we'll walk him up and down—keep him a-going—that's his only salvation! Oh! John, John! that ever your bashfulness should drive you into this! Up with him, father! Oh! he's dying! He ain't able to help himself one bit!"

They dragged me off the bed, and marched me up and down the room. Supposing, as a matter of course, that I ought to be expiring, I felt that I was expiring. My knees tottered under me; they only hauled me around the more violently. They forced a spoonful of tartar-emetic down my throat; Mary, the servant-girl, poured a quart of black coffee down me, half outside and half in; then they jerked me about the floor again, as if we were dancing a Virginia reel.

The doctor came and poked a long rubber tube down and converted me into a patent pump, until the tartar-emetic, and the coffee, and the pumpkin-pie I had eaten for dinner had all revisited this mundane sphere.

They had no mercy on me; I promenaded up and down and across with father, with Mary, with the doctor, until I felt that I should die if they didn't allow me to stop promenading.

The worst of it was, the house was full of folks; they crowded about the chamber door and looked at me, dancing up and down with the hired girl and the doctor.

"Shut the door—they shall *not* look at me!" I gasped, at last. The doctor felt my pulse and said proudly to my mother:

"Madam, your son will live! Our skill and vigilance have saved him."

"Bless you, doctor!" sobbed my parents.

"I will *not* live," I moaned, "to be the laughing stock of Babbletown. I will buy some more."

"John," said my father, weeping, "arouse yourself! You shall leave this place, if you desire it—only live! I will get you the position of weather-gauger on top of Mount Washington, if you say so, but don't commit any more suicide, my son!"

I was affected, and promised that I wouldn't, provided that I was found a situation somewhere by myself. So the excitement subsided. Father slept with me that night, keeping one eye open; the doctor got the credit of saving my life, and the girls of Babbletown were scared out of laughing at me for a whole month.

When we came to talk the matter over seriously—father and I—it was found to be too late in the season to procure me the Mount Washington appointment for the winter; besides, the effect of my attempt to "shuffle off this mortal coil" was to literally overrun our store with customers. People came from the country for fifteen miles around, in ox teams, on horse-back, in sleighs and cutters, and bob-sleds, and crockery-crates, to buy something, in hopes of getting a glimpse of the bashful young man who swallowed the pizen. Now, father was too cute a Yankee not to take advantage of the mob. He forgot his promises, and made me stay in the store from morning till night, so that women could say: "I bought this 'ere shirting from the young man who committed suicide; he did it up with his own hands."

"I'll give you a fair share o' the profits, John," father would say, slyly.

Well, things went on as it greased; the girls mostly stayed away—the Babbletown girls, for they had guilty consciences, I suspect; and in February there came a thaw. I stood looking out of the store window one day; the snow had melted in the street, and right over the stones that had been laid across the road for a walk, there was a great puddle of muddy water about two yards wide and a foot deep. I soon saw Hetty Slocum tripping across the street; she came to the puddle and stood still; the soft slush was heaped up on either side— she couldn't get around and she couldn't go through. My natural gallantry got the better of my resentment, and I went out to help her over, notwithstanding what she had said when I was under the counter. Planting one foot firmly in the center of the puddle and bracing the other against the curb-stone, I extended my hand.

"If you're good at jumping, Miss Slocum," said I, "I'll land you safely on this side."

"Oh," said she, roguishly, "Mr. Flutter, can I trust you?" and she reached out her little gloved hand.

All my old embarrassment rushed over me. I became nervous at the critical moment when I should have been cool. I never could tell just how it happened—whether her glove was slippery, or my foot slipped on a piece of ice under slush, or what—but the next moment we were both of us sitting down in fourteen inches of very cold, very muddy water.

My best beaver hat flew off and was run over by a passing sled, while a little dog ran away with Hetty's seal-skin muff.

I floundered around in that puddle for about two minutes, and then I got up. Hetty still sat there. She was white, she was so mad.

"I might a known better," said she. "Let me alone. I'd sit here forever, before I'd let *you* help me up."

THE NEXT MOMENT WE WERE BOTH OF US SITTING DOWN IN FOURTEEN INCHES OF VERY COLD, VERY MUDDY WATER.

The boys were coming home from school, and they began to hoot and laugh. I ran after the little dog who was making off with the muff. How Hetty got up, or who came to her rescue I don't know. That cur belonged about four miles out of town, and he never let up until he got home.

I grabbed the muff just as he was disappearing under the house with it, and then I walked slowly back. The people who didn't know me took me for an escaped convict—I was water-soaked and muddy, hatless, and had a sneaking expression, like that of a convicted horse-thief. Two or three persons attempted to arrest me. Finally, two stout farmers succeeded, and brought me into the village in triumph, and marched me between them to the jail.

"Why, what's Mr. Flutter been doin'?" asked the sheriff, coming out to meet us.

"Do you mean to say you know him?" inquired one of the men.

"Yes, I know him. That's our esteemed fellow-citizen, young Flutter."

"And he ain't no horse-thief nor nuthin'!"

"Not a bit of it, I assure you."

The man eyed me from head to foot, critically and contemptuously.

"Then all I've got to say," he remarked slowly, "is this—appearances is very deceptive."

It was getting dusk by this time, and I was thankful for it.

"I slipped down in a mud-puddle and lost my hat," I explained to the sheriff, as I turned away, and had the satisfaction of hearing the other one of my arresters say, behind my back:

"Oh, drunk!"

I hired a little boy, for five cents, to deliver Miss Slocum's muff at her residence. Then I went into the house by the kitchen, bribed Mary to clean my soiled pants without telling mother, slipped up-stairs, and went to bed without my supper.

The next day I bought a handsome seven-dollar ring, and sent it to Hetty as some compensation for the damage done to her dress.

That evening was singing-school evening. I went early, so as to get my seat without attracting attention. Early as I was, I was not the first. A group of young people was gathered about the great black-board, on which the master illustrated his lessons. They were having lots of fun, and did not notice me as I came in. I stole quietly to a seat behind a pillar. Fred Hencoop was drawing something on the board, and explaining it. As he drew back and pointed with the long stick, I saw a splendid caricature of myself pursuing a small dog with a muff, while a young lady sat quietly in a mud-puddle in the corner of the black-board, and Fred was saying, with intense gravity:

"This is the man, all tattered and torn, that spattered the maiden all forlorn. *This* is the dog that stole the muff. *This* is the ring he sent the maid—"

"Muff-in ring," suggested some one, and then they laughed louder than ever.

I felt that that singing-school was no place for me that evening, and I stole away as noiselessly as I had entered.

I went home and packed my trunk. The next morning I said to father:

"Give me my share of the profits for the last month," and he gave me one hundred and thirty dollars. "I am going where no one knows me, mother, so good-bye. You'll hear from me when I'm settled," and I was actually off on the nine o'clock New York express.

Every seat was full in every car but one—one seat beside a pretty, fashionably-dressed young lady was vacant. I stood up against the wood-box and looked at that seat, as a boy looks at a jar of peppermint-drops in a candy-store window. After a while I reflected that these people were all strangers, and, of course, unaware of my infirmity; this gave me a certain degree of courage. I left the support of the wood-box and made my way along the aisle until I came to the vacant seat.

"Miss," I began, politely, but the lady purposely looked the other way; she had her bag in the place where I wanted to sit, and she didn't mean to move it, if she could help it. "Miss," I said again, in a louder tone.

Two or three people looked at us. That confused me; her refusing to look around confused me; one of my old bad spells began to come on.

"Miss," I whispered, leaning toward her, blushing and embarrassed, "I would like to know if you are engaged—if—if you are taken, I mean?"

She looked at me then sharp enough.

"Yes, sir, I *am*," she said calmly; "and going to be married next week."

The passengers began to laugh, and I began to back out. I didn't stop at the wood-box, but retreated into the next car, where I stood until my legs ached, and then sat down by an ancient lady, with a long nose, blue spectacles, and a green veil.

CHAPTER VII.

I MAKE A NARROW ESCAPE.

It is a serious thing to be as bashful as I am. There's nothing at all funny about it, though some people seem to think there is. I was assured, years ago, that it would wear off and betray the brass underneath; but I must have been triple-plated. I have had rubs enough to wear out a wash-board, yet there doesn't a bit of brass come to the surface yet. Beauty may be only skin-deep; modesty, like mine, pervades the grain. If I really believed my bashfulness was only cuticle-deep, I'd be flayed to-day, and try and grow a hardier complexion without any Bloom of Youth in it. No use! I could pave a ten-thousand-acre prairie with the "good intentions" I have wasted, the firm resolutions I have broken. Born to be bashful is only another way of expressing the Bible truth, "Born to trouble as the sparks are to fly upward."

When I sat down by the elderly lady in the railway train, I felt comparatively at ease. She was older than mother, and I didn't mind her rather aggressive looks and ways; in short, I seemed to feel that in case of necessity she would protect me. Not that I was afraid of anything, but she would probably at least keep me from proposing to any more young ladies. Alas! how *could* I have any presentiment of the worse danger lurking in store for me? How could I, young, innocent, and inexperienced, foresee the unforeseeable? I could not. Reviewing all the circumstances by the light of wiser days, I still deny that I was in any way, shape, or manner to blame for what occurred. I sat in my half of the seat, occupying as little room as possible, my eyes fixed on the crimson plush cushions of the seat before me, my thoughts busy with the mortifying past, and the great unknown future into which I was blindly rushing at the rate of thirty miles an hour—sat there, dreading the great city into which I was so soon to plunge—when a voice, closely resembling vinegar sweetened with honey, said, close to my ear:

"Goin' to New York, sir?"

"Yes, ma'am," I answered, coming out of my reverie with a little jump.

"I'm real glad," said my companion, taking off her blue spectacles, and leaning toward me confidentially; "so I am. I'm quite unprotected, sir, quite, and I shall be thankful to place myself under your care. I'm goin' down to the city to buy my spring stock o' millinery, an' any little attention you can show me will be gratefully received—gratefully. I don't mind admitting to *you*, young man, for you look pure and uncorrupted, that I am terribly afraid of men. They are wicked, heartless creatures. I feel that I might more safely trust myself with ravening wolves than with men in general, but *you* are different. *You* have had a good mother."

"Yes, ma'am, I have," I responded, rather warmly.

I was pleased at her commendation of me and mother, but puzzled as to the character of the danger to which she referred. I finally concluded that she was afraid of being robbed, and I put my lips close to her ear, so that no one should overhear us, and asked:

"Do you carry your money about you?—you ought not to run such a risk. I've been told there are always one or more thieves on every express train."

"My dear young friend," she whispered back, very, very close in my ear, "I was not thinking of money—*that* is all in checks, safely deposited in—in—in te-he! inside the lining of my waist. I was only referring to the dangers which ever beset the unmarried lady, especially the unsophisticated maiden, far, far from her native village. Why, would you believe it, already, sir, since I left home, a man, a *gentleman*, sitting in the very seat where you sit now, made love to me, out-and-out!"

"Made love to you?" I stammered, shrinking into the farthest corner, and regarding her with undisguised astonishment.

"You may well appear surprised. Promise me that you will remain by my side until we reach our destination."

She appeared kind of nervous and agitated, and I promised. Instead of being protected, I found myself figuring in the *role* of protector. My timid companion did the most of the talking; she pumped me pretty dry of facts about myself, and confided to me that she was doing a good business—making eight hundred a year clear profit— and all she wanted to complete her satisfaction was the right kind of a partner.

She proposed to me to become that partner. I said that I did not understand the millinery business; she said I had been a clerk in a dry-goods store, and that was the first step; I said I didn't think I should fancy the bonnet line. She said I should be a *silent* partner; all in the world I'd have to do would be to post the books, and she'd warrant me a thousand dollars a year, for the business would double. I said I had but one hundred and thirty dollars; she said, write to my pa for more, but she'd take me without a cent—there was something in my face that showed her I was to be trusted.

She was so persistent that I began to be alarmed—I felt that I should be drawn into that woman's clutches against my will. I got pale and cold, and the perspiration broke out on my brow. Was it for this I had fled from home and friends? To become a partner in the hat-and-bonnet business, with a dreadful old maid, who wore blue spectacles and curled her false hair. I shivered.

"Poor darling!" said she, "the boy is cold," and she wrapped me up in a big plaid shawl of her own.

The very touch of that shawl made me feel as if I had a thousand caterpillars crawling over me; yet I was too bashful to break loose from its folds. I grew feverish.

"There," said she, "you are getting your color back."

The more attention she paid to me the more homesick I grew. I looked piteously in the conductor's face as he passed by. He smiled relentlessly. I glanced wildly yet furtively about to see if, perchance, a vacant seat were to be described.

"Rest thy head on this shoulder; thou art weary," she said. "I will put my veil over your face and you can catch a nap."

But I was not to be caught napping.

"No, I thank you—I never sleep in the day time," I stammered.

Oh, what a ride I was having! How wretched I felt! Yet I was too bashful to shake off the shawl and stand up before a car-load of people.

Suddenly, something happened. The blue spectacles flew over my head, and I flew over the seat in front of me. Thank goodness! I was saved from that female! I picked myself up from out of the *débris* of the wreck. I saw a green veil, and a lady looking around for her lost teeth, and having ascertained that no one was killed, I limped away and hid behind a stump. I stayed behind that stump three mortal hours. When the train went again on its winding way I was not one of the passengers. I walked, bruised and sore as I was, to the nearest village, and took the first train in the opposite direction. That evening, as father and mother were sitting down to their solitary but excellent tea, I walked in on 'em.

"No more foreign trips for me," said I; "I will stick to Babbletown, and try and stand the consequences."

About four days after this, father laid a letter on the counter before me—a large, long, yellow envelope, with a big red seal. "Read that," was his brief comment.

I took it up, unfolded the foolscap, and read:

"JOHN FLUTTER, SENIOR:—I have the honor to inform you that my client, Miss Alvira Slimmens, has instructed me to proceed against your son for breach of promise of marriage, laying her damages at twelve hundred dollars. As your son is not legally of age, we shall hold you responsible. A compromise, to avoid publicity of suit, is possible. Send us your check for $1,000 and you will hear no more of this matter.

"Respectfully,

"WILLIAM BLACK, Attorney-at-Law,

"*Pennyville, N. Y.*"

"Oh, father!" I cried, "I swear to you this is not my fault!" Looking up in distress I saw that my parent was laughing.

"I have heard of Alvira before," said he; "no, it is *not* your fault, my poor boy. Let me see, Alvira was thirty twenty-one years ago when I was married to your ma. I used to be in Pennyville sometimes, in those days, and she was sweet on me, John, then. I'll answer this letter, and answer it to her, and not her lawyer. Don't you be uneasy, my son. I'll tend to her. But you had a narrow escape; I don't wonder you, with your bashfulness, fled homeward to your ma."

"Then it wasn't my blunder this time, father?"

"I exonerate you, my son!"

For once a glow of happiness diffused itself over my much-tried spirits. I was so exalted that when a young lady came in for a bottle of bandoline I gave her Spaulding's prepared glue instead; and the next time I met that young lady she wore a bang—she had used the new-fangled bandoline, and the only way to get the stuff out of her hair was to cut it off.

CHAPTER VIII.

HE ENACTS THE PART OF GROOMSMAN.

"Out of the frying-pan into the fire!" This should have been my chosen motto from the beginning. The performance of the maddening feat indicated in the proverb has been the principal business of my life. I am always finding myself in the frying-pan, and always flopping out into the fire. My father's interference saved me from the dreadful old creature into whose net I had stumbled when I fled from my native village, only to return with the certainty that I was unfit to cope with the world outside of it.

"I will never put my foot beyond the township line again," I vowed to my secret soul. I had a harrowing sorrow preying upon me all the remainder of the winter. I was given to understand that Belle Marigold was actually engaged to Fred Hencoop. And she might have been mine! Alas, that mighty *might*!

"Of all sad words of tongue or pen
The saddest are these—'It might have been!'"

I am positive that when I first came home from school she admired me very much. She welcomed my early attentions. It was only the ridiculous blunders into which my bashfulness continually drove me that alienated her regard. If I had not caught my foot in the reins that time I got out of the buggy in front of her house—if I had not fallen in the water and had my clothes shrink in drying—nor choked almost to death—nor got under the counter—nor failed to "speak my piece"—nor sat down in that mud-puddle—nor committed suicide—nor run away from home—nor performed any other of the thousand-and-one absurd feats into which my constitutional embarrassment was everlastingly urging me, I declare boldly, "Belle might have been mine." She had encouraged me at first. Now it was too late. She had "declined," as Tennyson says, "on a lower love than mine"—on Fred Hencoop's.

45

The thought was despair. Never did I realized of what the human heart is capable until Belle came into the store, one lovely spring morning, looking like a seraph in a new spring bonnet, and blushingly—with a saucy flash of her dark eyes that made her rising color all the more divine—inquired for table-damask and 4-4 sheetings.

With an ashen brow and quivering lip, I displayed before her our best assortment of table-cloths and napkins, pillow-casing and sheeting. Her mother accompanied her to give her the benefit of her experience; and kept telling her daughter to choose the best, and what and how many dozens she had before she was married.

They ran up a big bill at the store that morning, and father came behind the counter to help, and was mightily pleased; but I felt as if I were measuring off cloth for my own shroud.

"Come, John, you go do up the sugar for Widow Smith, her boy is waiting," said my parent, seeing the muddle into which I was getting things. "I will attend to these ladies—twelve yards of the pillow-casing, did you say, Mrs. Marigold?"

I moved down to the end of the store and weighed and tied up in brown paper the "three pounds of white sugar to make cake for the sewin'-society," which the lad had asked for. A little girl came in for a pound of bar-soap, and I attended to her wants. Then another boy, with a basket, came in a hurry for a dozen of eggs. You see, ours was one of those village-stores that combine all things.

While I waited on these insignificant customers father measured off great quantities of white goods for the two ladies; and I strained my ears to hear every word that was said. They asked father if he was going to New York *soon*? He said, in about ten days. Then Mrs. Marigold confided to him that they wanted him to purchase twenty-five yards of white corded silk.

If every cord in that whole piece of silk had been drawing about my throat I couldn't have felt more suffocated. I sat right down, I felt so faint, in a tub of butter. I had just sense enough left to remember that

I had on my new spring lavender pants. The butter was disgustingly soft and mushy.

"Come here, John, and add up this bill," called father.

"I can't; I'm sick."

I had got up from the tub and was leaning on the counter—I was pale, I know.

"Why, what's the matter?" he asked.

Belle cast one guilty look in my direction. "It's the spring weather, I dare say," she said softly to my parent.

I sneaked out of the back door and went across the yard to the house to change my pants. I *was* sick, and I did not emerge from my room until the dinner-bell rang.

I went down then, and found father, usually so good-natured, looking cross, as he carved the roast beef.

"You will never be good for anything, John," was his salutation—"at least, not as a clerk. I've a good mind to write to Captain Hall to take you to the North Pole."

"What's up, father?"

"Oh, nothing!" *very* sarcastically. "That white sugar you sent Mrs. Smith was table-salt, and she made a whole batch of cake out of it before she discovered her mistake. She was out of temper when she flew in the store, I tell you. I had not only to give her the sugar, but enough butter and eggs to make good her loss, and throw in a neck-tie to compensate her for waste of time. Before she got away, in came the mother of the little girl to whom you had given a slab of molasses candy for bar-soap, and said that the child had brought nothing home but some streaks of molasses on her face. Just as I was coming out to dinner the other boy brought back the porcelain eggs you had given him with word that 'Ma had biled 'em an hour, and she couldn't even budge the shells.' So you see, my son, that in a miscellaneous store you are quite out of your element."

"It was that flirt of a Belle Marigold that upset him," said mother, laughing so that she spilled the gravy on the table-cloth. "He'll be all right when she is once Mrs. Hencoop."

That very evening Fred came in the store to ask me to be his groomsman.

"We're going to be married the first of June," he told me, grinning like an idiot.

"Does Belle know that you invite me to be groomsman?" I responded, gloomily.

"Yes; she suggested that you be asked. Rose Ellis is to be bridesmaid."

"Very well; I accept."

"All right, old fellow. Thank you," slapping me on the back.

As I lay tossing restlessly on my bed that night—after an hour spent in a vain attempt to take the butter out of my lavenders with French chalk—I made a new and firm resolution. I would make Belle sorry that she had given her preference to Fred. I would so bear myself— during our previous meetings and consultations, and during the day of the ceremony—that she should bitterly repent not having given me an opportunity to conquer my diffidence before taking up with Frederick Hencoop. The opportunity was given me to redeem myself. I would prove that, although modest, I was a gentleman; that the blushing era of inexperience could be succeeded by one of calm grandeur. Chesterfield could never have been more quietly self-possessed; Beau Brummell more imperturbable. I would get by heart all the little formalities of the occasion, and, when the time came, I would execute them with consummate ease.

These resolutions comforted me—supported me under the weight of despair I had to endure. Ha! yes. I would show some people that some things could be done as well as others.

It was four weeks to the first of June. As I had ruined my lavender trousers I ordered another pair, with suitable neck-tie, vest, and gloves, from New York. I also ordered three different and lately-published books on etiquette. I studied in all three of these the etiquette of weddings. I thoroughly posted myself on the ancient, the present, and the future duties of "best men" on such occasions. I learned how they do it in China, in Turkey, in Russia, in New Zealand, more particularly how it is done, at present, in England and America. As the day drew nigh I felt equal to the emergency I had a powerful motive for acquitting myself handsomely. I wanted to show *her* what a mistake she had made.

The wedding was to take place in church at eight o'clock in the evening. The previous evening we—that is, the bride-elect, groom, bridesmaid, and groomsman, parents, and two or three friends—had a private rehearsal, one of the friends assuming the part of clergyman. All went merry as a marriage bell. I was the soul of ease and grace: Fred was the awkward one, stepping on the bride's train, dropping the ring, and so forth.

"I declare, Mr. Flutter, I never saw any one improve as you have," said Belle, aside to me, when we had returned to her house. "I do hope poor Fred will get along better to-morrow. I shall be really vexed at him if anything goes wrong."

"You must forgive a little flustration on his part," I loftily answered. "Perhaps, were I in his place, I should be agitated too."

Well, the next evening came, and at seven o'clock I repaired to the squire's residence. Fred was already there, walking up and down the parlor, a good deal excited, but dressed faultlessly and looking frightfully well.

"Why, John," was his first greeting, "aren't you going to wear any cravat?"

I put my hand up to my neck and dashed madly back a quarter of a mile for the delicate white silk tie I had left on my dressing bureau. This, of course, made me uncomfortably warm. When I got back to the squire's I was in a perspiration, felt that my calm brow was flushed, and had to wipe it with my handkerchief.

"Come," said that impatient Fred, "you have just two minutes to get your gloves on."

My hands were damp, and being hurried had the effect to make me nervous, in spite of four long weeks' constant resolution. What with the haste and perspiration, I tore the thumb completely out of the left glove.

Never mind; no time to mend, in spite of the proverb.

The bride came down-stairs, cool, white, and delicious as an orange blossom. She was helped into one carriage; Fred and I entered another.

"I hope you feel cool," I said to Fred.

"I hope *you* do," he retorted.

I have always laid the catastrophe which followed to the first mistake in having to fly home for my neck-tie. I was disconcerted by that, and I couldn't exactly get concerted again.

I don't know what happened after the carriage stopped at the church door—I must take the report of my friends for it. They say that I bolted at the last moment, and followed the bride up one aisle instead of the groom up the other, as I should have done. But I was perfectly calm and collected. Oh, yes, that was why, when we attempted to form in front of the altar, I insisted on standing next to Belle, and when I was finally pushed into my place by the irate Fred, I kept diving forward every time the clergyman said anything, trying to take the bride's hand, and responding, "Belle, I take thee to be my lawful, wedded," answering, "I do," loudly, to every question, even to that "Who gives this woman?" etc., until every man, woman, and child in church was tittering and giggling, and the holy man had to come to a full pause, and request me to realize that it was not I who was being married.

"I do. With all my worldly goods I thee endow," was my reply to his reminder.

"For Heaven's sake subside, or I'll thrash you within an inch of your life when I get out of this," whispered Fred.

Dimly mistrusting that I was on the wrong track, I turned and seized Mrs. Marigold by the hand, and began to feel in my pocket for a ring, because I saw the groom taking one out of his pocket.

The giggling and tittering increased; somebody—father or the constable—took me by the shoulder and marched me out of that; after which, I suppose, the ceremony was duly concluded. I only know that somebody knocked me down about five minutes afterward—I have been told that it was the bridegroom who did it— and that all the books of etiquette on earth won't fortify a man against the attacks of constitutional bashfulness.

CHAPTER IX.

MEETS A PAIR OF BLUE EYES.

I kept pretty quiet the remainder of that summer—didn't even attend church for several weeks. In fact, I got father to give me a vacation, and beat a retreat into the country during the month of July, to an aunt of mine, who lived on a small farm with her husband, her son of fourteen, and a "hand." Their house was at least a mile from the nearest neighbor's, and as I was less afraid of Aunt Jerusha than of any other being of her sex, and as there was not another frock, sun-bonnet, or apron within the radius of a mile, I promised myself a month of that negative bliss which comes from retrospection, solitude, and the pleasure of following the men about the harvest-field. Sitting quietly under some shadowing tree, with my line cast into the still pool of a little babbling trout-brook, where it was held in some hollow of nature's hand, I had leisure to forget the past and to make good resolutions for the future. Belle Marigold was forever lost to me. She was Mrs. Hencoop; and Fred had knocked me down because I had been so unfortunate as to lose my presence of mind at his wedding. All was over between us.

The course now open for me to pursue was to forever steel my heart to the charms of the other sex, to attend strictly to business, to grow rich and honored, while, at the same time, I hardened into a sort of granite obelisk, incapable of blushing, faltering, or stepping on other people's toes.

One day, as the men were hauling in the "loaded wains" from the fields to the great barn, I sat under my favorite tree, as usual, waiting for a bite. Three speckled beauties already lay in a basin of water at my side, and I was thinking what a pleasant world this would be were there no girls in it, when suddenly I heard a burst of silvery laughter!

Looking up, there, on the opposite side of the brook, stood two young ladies! They were evidently city girls. Their morning toilets were the perfection of simple elegance—hats, parasols, gloves, dresses, the very cream of style.

Both of them were pretty—one a dark, bright-eyed brunette, the other a blonde, fair as a lily and sweet as a rose. Their faces sparkled with mischief, but they made a great effort to resume their dignity.

I jumped to my feet, putting one of them—my feet, I mean—in the basin of water I had for my trout.

"Oh, it's too bad to disturb you, sir," said the dark-eyed one. "You were just having a nibble, I do believe. But we have lost our way. We are boarding at the Widow Cooper's, and came out for a ramble in the woods, and got lost; and here, just as we thought we were on the right way home, we came to this naughty little river, or whatever you call it, and can't go a step farther. Is there no way of getting across it, sir?"

"There is a bridge about a quarter of a mile above here, but to get to it you will have to go through a field in which there is a very cross bull. Then there is a log just down here a little ways—I'll show it to you, ladies"; and tangling my beautiful line inextricably in my embarrassment, I threw down my fishing-rod and led the way, I on one side of the stream and they on the other.

"Oh, oh!" cried Blue-Eyes, when we reached the log. "I'll be sure to get dizzy and fall off."

"Nonsense!" said Black-Eyes, bravely, and walked over without winking.

"I shall never—never dare!" screamed Blue-Eyes.

"Allow me to assist you, miss," I said, in my best style, going on the log and reaching out my hand to steady her.

She laid her little gray glove in my palm, and put one tiny slipper on the log, and then she stood, the little coquette! shrinking and laughing, and taking a step and retreating, and I falling head over ears in love with her, deeper and deeper every second. I do believe, if the other one hadn't been there, I would have taken her right up in

53

my arms and carried her over. Well, Black-Eyes began to scold, and so, at last, she ventured across, and then she said she was tired and thirsty, and did wish she had a glass of milk; and so I asked her to go to the house, and rest a few minutes, and Aunt Jerusha would give them some milk. You'd better believe aunt opened her eyes, when she saw me marching in as bold as brass, with two stylish young ladies; while, the moment I met her sly look, all my customary confusion—over which I had contrived to hold a tight rein—ran rampant and jerked at my self-possession until I lost control of it!

"These young ladies, Aunt Jerusha," I stammered, "would like a glass of milk. They've got lost, and don't know where they are, and can't find their way back, and I expect I'll have to show them the way."

"They're very welcome," said aunt, who was kindness itself, and she went into the milk-pantry and brought out two large goblets of morning's milk, with the rising cream sticking around the inside.

I started forward gallantly, took the server from aunt's hand, and conveyed it, with almost the grace of a French waiter, across the large kitchen to where the two beautiful beings were resting in the chairs which I had set for them. Unfortunately, being blinded by my bashfulness, I caught my toe in a small hole in aunt's rag carpet, the result being that I very abruptly deposited both glasses of milk, bottom up, in the lap of Blue-Eyes. A feeling of horror overpowered me as I saw that exquisite toilet in ruins—those dainty ruffles, those cunning bows the color of her eyes, submerged in the lacteal fluid.

I think a ghastly pallor must have overspread my face as I stood motionless, grasping the server in my clenched hands.

What do you think Blue-Eyes said? *This* is the way she "gave me fits." Looking up prettily to my aunt, she says:

"Oh, madam, I am *so* sorry for your carpet."

"Your dress!" exclaimed Aunt Jerusha.

"Never mind *that*, madam. It can go to the laundry."

"Well, I never!" continued aunt, flying about for a towel, and wiping her off as well as she could; "but John Flutter is so careless. He's *always* blundering. He means well enough, but he's bashful. You'd think a clerk in a dry-goods store would get over it some time now, wouldn't you? Well, young ladies, I'll get some more milk for you; but I won't trust it in *his* hands."

When Aunt Jerusha let the cat out of the bag about my bashfulness, Blue-Eyes flashed, at me from under her long eyelashes a glance so roguish, so perfectly infatuating, that my heart behaved like a thermometer that is plunged first into a tea-kettle and then into snow; it went up into my throat, and then down into my boots. I still grasped the server and stood there like a revolving lantern—one minute white, another red. Finally my heart settled into my boots. It was evident that fate was against me. I was *doomed* to go on leading a blundering existence. My admiration for this lovely girl was already a thousand times stronger than any feeling I had ever had for Belle Marigold. Yet how ridiculous I must appear to her. How politely she was laughing at me.

The sense of this, and the certainty that I was born to blunder, came home to me with crushing weight. I turned slowly to Aunt Jerusha, who was bringing fresh milk, and said, with a simplicity to which pathos must have given dignity:

"Aunt, will you show them the way to Widow Cooper's? I am going to the barn to hang myself," and I walked out.

"Is he in earnest?" I heard Blue-Eyes inquire.

"Wall, now, I shouldn't be surprised," avowed Aunt Jerusha. "He's been powerful low-spirited lately. You see, ladies, he was born that bashful that life is a burden to him."

I walked on in the direction of the barn; I would not pause to listen or to cast a backward glance. Doubtless, my relative told them of my previous futile attempt to poison myself—perhaps became so interested in relating anecdotes of her nephew's peculiar temperament, that she forgot the present danger which threatened him. At least, it was some time before she troubled herself to follow me to ascertain if my threat meant anything serious.

When she finally arrived at the large double door, standing wide open for the entrance of the loaded wagons, she gave a sudden shriek.

"I STOOD READY FOR THE FATAL LEAP."

I was standing on the beam which supported the light flooring of the hay-loft; beneath was the threshing-floor; above me the great rafters of the barn, and around one of these I had fastened a rope, the other terminus of which was knotted about my neck.

I stood ready for the fatal leap.

As she screamed, I slightly raised my hand:

"Silence, Aunt Jerusha, and receive my parting instructions. Tell Blue-Eyes that I love her madly, but not to blame herself for my untimely end. The ruin of her dress was only the last drop in the cup—the last straw on the camel's back. Farewell!" and as she threw up her arms and shrieked to me to desist, I rolled up my eyes—and sprang from the beam.

For a moment I thought myself dead. The experience was different from what I had anticipated. Instead of feeling choked, I had a pain in my legs, and it seemed to me that I had been shut together like an opera-glass. Still I knew that I must be dead, and I kept very quiet until the sound of little screams and gurgles of—what?—*laughter,* smote my ears!

Then I opened my eyes and looked about. I was not dangling in the air overhead, but standing on the threshing-floor, with a bit of broken halter about my neck. The rope had played traitor and given way without even chafing my throat.

I dare say the sight of me, standing there with my eyes closed and looking fully convinced that I was dead, must have been vastly amusing to the two young ladies, who had followed Aunt Jerusha to the door. They laughed as if I had been the prince of clowns, and had just performed a most funny trick in the ring. I began to feel as if I had, too.

Aunt rushed forward and gave me a shake.

"Another blunder, John," she said; "it's plain as the nose on a man's face that Providence never intended you to commit suicide."

And then Blue-Eyes, repressing her mirth, came forward, half shy and half coaxing, and said to me:

"How my sister and I would feel if you had killed yourself on our account! Come! do please show us the way to our boarding-house. Mamma will be so anxious about us."

Cunning witch! she knows, how to twist a man around her little finger.

"Come," she continued, "let *me* untie this ugly rope."

And I did let her, and picked up my hat to walk with them to the Widow Cooper's.

They made themselves very agreeable on the way—so that I would think no more of hanging myself, I suppose.

Only one more little incident occurred on the road. We met a tramp. He was a roughly-dressed fellow, with a straw hat such as farmers wear, whose broad brim nearly hid his face. He sauntered up impudently, and, before we could pass him, he chucked Blue-Eyes under the chin. In less than half a second he was flying backward over the rail fence, although he was a tall fellow, more than my weight.

"Now," said I proudly to myself, "she will forget that unlucky circus performance in the barn."

Imagine my sensations when she turned on me with the fire flashing out of those soft blue eyes.

"What did you fling my brother over the fence for?"

That was what she asked me.

CHAPTER X.

HE CATCHES A TROUT AND PRESENTS IT TO A LADY.

"Some achieve greatness; some have greatness thrust upon them." I think I have achieved greatness. Of one thing I am convinced: that it is only necessary to do some one thing *well*—as well or better than any one else—in order to acquire distinction. The thing I do really well—better than any living human being—is to blunder. I defy competition. There are champion tight-rope dancers, billiard players, opera singers, swindlers, base-ballists, candidates for the Presidency. I am the champion blunderer. You remember the man who asked of another, "Who is that coarse, homely creature across the room?" and received for answer, "That creature is my wife!" Well, I *ought* to have been that man, although in that case I did not happen to be. My compliments always turn out to be left-handed ones; all my remarks, all my efforts to please are but so many never-ending *faux-pas*.

As a general seeks to retrieve one defeat by some act of unparalleled bravery, so had I sought to wipe out from the memory of the lovely pair whom I escorted, my shameful failure to hang myself, by gallantly pitching over the fence the fellow who had made himself too familiar with the fairer of the two; and, as a *matter of course*, he turned out to be her favorite brother.

He was a good-natured fellow, after all—a perfect gentleman; and when I stammered out my excuses, saying that I had mistaken him for a tramp, he laughed and shook hands with me, explaining that he was in his fishing costume, and saying very handsomely that were his dear sister ever in such danger of being insulted, he hoped some person as plucky as I would be on hand to defend her. This was applying cold cream to my smarting self-love. But it did not prevent me from observing the sly glances exchanged between the girls, nor prevent my hearing the little bursts of suppressed giggling which they pretended were caused by the funny motions of the hay-cutter in a neighboring field. So, as their brother could show them the way to Widow Cooper's, I said good-morning rather abruptly. He called me back, however, and asked if I would not like to join him on a fishing tramp in the morning. I said "I would, and I knew all the best places."

Then we shook hands again, while the young ladies smiled like angels; but I had not more than turned a bend in the road, which hid me from view, than I heard such shrieks and screams of laughter as turned my two ears into boiled lobsters for the remainder of the day.

But, spite of my burning ears, I could not get mad at those girls. They had a right to laugh at me, for I had, as usual, made myself ridiculous. I was head over ears in love with Blue-Eyes. The feeling I had once cherished toward Belle Marigold, compared with my sudden adoration of this glorious stranger, was as bean-soup to the condensed extract of beef, as water to wine, as milk to cream, as mush to mince-pie.

I do not think I slept a wink that night. My room was suffocating, and I took a pillow, and crawled out on the roof of the kitchen, just under my window, and stretched myself out on the shingles, and winked back at the stars which winked at me, and thought of the bright, flashing eyes of the bewitching unknown. I resolved to seek her acquaintance, through her brother, and never, never to blunder again, but to be calm and cool like other young men—calm, cool, and persistent. It might have been four o'clock in the morning that I came to this determination, and so soothing was it, that I was able to take a brief nap after it.

I was awakened by young Knickerbocker, the lady's brother, tickling the soles of my feet with a rake, and I started up with such violence from a sound sleep, that I slipped on the inclined plane, rolled down to the edge, and went over into a hogshead of rain-water just underneath.

"A capital way to take your morning bath," smiled Knickerbocker. "Come, Mr. Flutter, get out of that, and find your rod and line, and come along. I have a good breakfast in this basket, which we will eat in some dewy nook of the woods, while we are waiting for a nibble. The early bird catches the worm, you know."

"I'll be with you in a moment," I answered with a blank grin, determined to be cool and composed, though my sudden plunge had somewhat dazed me; and scrambling out of the primitive cistern, I regained the roof by means of a ladder standing against a cherry-tree not far away.

Consoling myself with the idea that this early adventure was an *accident* and not a *blunder*, I hastily dressed, and rejoined my new friend, with rod and line, and a box of flies.

We had a delightful morning. Knickerbocker was affable. Alone in the solitudes of nature with one of my own sex, I was tolerably at home, and flattered myself that I appeared to considerable advantage, especially as I really was a skillful angler, and landed two trout to my friend's landing one. By ten o'clock we each had a lovely string of the speckled beauties, and decided to go home for the day, returning on the morrow.

The path we took out of the woods came into the highway just in front of the Widow Cooper's. I knew it, but I felt quite cool, and determined to make some excuse to catch another glimpse of my companion's sister. I had one splendid fish among my treasures, weighing over two pounds, while none of his weighed over a pound. I would present that trout to Flora Knickerbocker! I would ask her to have the cook prepare it for her special delectation.

We emerged upon the lawn and sauntered up to the front of the house, where some half-dozen ladies were sitting on the long porch, doing worsted-work and reading novels. I saw my charmer among them, and, as she looked up from the book she was reading, and shot at me a mischievous glance from those thrilling eyes, I felt my coolness melting at the most alarming rate.

How I envied the easy, careless grace with which my friend sauntered up to the group! Why should I not be as graceful, as easy? I would make a desperate effort to "assume a virtue if I had it not." I, too, sauntered elegantly, lifted my hat killingly, and approached my charmer just as if I didn't realize that I was turning all the colors of the chameleon.

"Miss Knickerbocker," I began, "will you deign to accept the champion trout of the season?"

The string of glistening fish hung from the fine patent rod which I carried over my shoulder. I never could undo the tangle of how it all came about; but, in my embarrassment, I must have handled things not quite so gracefully as I intended—the line had become unwound, and the hook dangling at the end of it as I attempted to lower the rod caught in my coat collar behind, and the more I tugged the more it would not come out. I flushed and jerked, and tried to see the back of my head, while the ladies smiled encouragingly, rendering me more and more desperate, until I gave a fearful twitch, and the barb came flying out and across the porch, striking a prim maiden lady on the head.

More and more confused, I gave a sudden pull to relieve the lady, and succeeded in getting a very queer bite indeed. At first I thought, in my horror, that I had drawn the whole top of the unfortunate spinster's head off; but a second frightened look showed me that it was only her scalpette, or false front, or whatever the dear creatures call a half-wig, all frizzes and crimps. Almost faint with dismay at the glare of anger in the lady's eyes, and the view of the bald white spot on top of her head, I hurriedly drew the thing toward me to remove it from the hook, when a confounded little Spitz, seeing the spot, and thinking, doubtless, I was playing with him, made a dash at the wig, and in less time than it takes to tell it, that thing of beauty was a wreck forever. Its unfortunate owner, with a look which nearly annihilated me, fled up-stairs to her apartment.

Nor was my discomfiture then ended. That Spitz—that precious Spitz—belonged to Blue-Eyes; I tried to coax him to relinquish his game; he would not be persuaded, and, in the ardor of his pursuit, he swallowed the cruel hook. I had wanted to present her with a trout, and had only succeeded in hooking her favorite pet—"her darling, her dear, dear little Spitzy-witzy," as she called him, in tones of mingled endearment and anguish, as she flew to rescue him from his cruel fate.

"Oh, what can I do?" she sobbed, looking up at her brother.

"Cut him open and remove the hook," he answered gravely; "there is no other possible way of relieving the poor fellow."

"I wish *I* had swallowed it," I murmured, bitterly, throwing my fish into the grass of the lawn, and pulling at my mustache desperately in my despair of ever doing as other people do.

"I really wish you had," snapped Blue-Eyes, satirically, and with that I walked off and left them to take Spitz from around that fish-hook the best way they could.

I don't imagine I left many female friends on that porch, nor did I see any of the Widow Cooper's boarders again for a week, when we were brought together, under rather peculiar circumstances at a circus.

CHAPTER XI.

HE GOES TO THE CIRCUS.

In vain I struggled to regain the peace of mind I was beginning to enjoy before I met Flora Knickerbocker. I could not forget her; I dared not approach her—for I had heard a rumor that her dog had died a *barb*-arous death, and his young mistress was inconsolable. I spent the long, lazy summer days in dreaming of her, and wishing that bashfulness were a curable disease.

One morning, very early, when

"The window slowly grew a glimmering square,"

I heard an unwonted commotion on our quiet road, and slipping out of bed, I went to the window to see "what was up." It was a circus company, with a menagerie attachment, winding through the dim dawn, elephant and all.

For a moment my heart beat, as in its childish days, at sight of the unique cavalcade; but it soon grew sad, and ached worse than ever at the reflection that Miss Flora was a city girl, and would despise a circus. However, some time during the day I heard from aunt that *all* of Widow Cooper's boarders had made up their minds to attend, that evening, the performance, which was to take place in a small town two miles from us. These fine city folks doubtless thought it would be an innocent "lark" to go to the circus in this obscure country village.

I had outgrown my childish taste for the hyena, the gnu, and the anaconda; I was indifferent to the india-rubber man; nor did I care much for the beautiful bare-back rider who was to flash through the hoops like a meteor through the orbits of the planets; but I did long to steal one more look, unseen, unsuspected, at the sweet face which was lovelier to me, even in its anger, than any other. I had been the means of Spitz's death—very well, I could hide myself in some obscure corner of the amphitheater, and gaze at her mournfully from the distance. While she gazed at the ring, I would gaze at *her*.

So I went to the circus, along with a good many other people. *She* came early with the Cooper party, and seemed interested and amused by the rough-board seats, and the novelty of the scene, and the audience. I had not yet chosen my perch on the boards, for I wanted to get as near to her as I could without her observing me.

The sight of her—resolved as I was to be cool, calm, and collected— so affected my eyesight that I walked right into the rope stretched around the ring, and fell over into the tan-bark.

All the boys hooted and laughed, and made personal remarks, wanting to know if I were the clown, and similar questions, which I heard with silent dignity. I hoped and prayed that *she* had not recognized the tumbler who had begun the performances as an amateur, and without any salary from Barnum. They were on the opposite side of the circle, and perhaps I escaped their remark.

Contriving to mingle myself with some newcomers, I made my way more cautiously to within a few feet of my charmer. I did not intend she should see me, and was surprised when she whispered to her brother, upon which he immediately looked in my direction and beckoned me to a seat in their party.

Oh, bliss! In another moment I was at her feet—sitting on the plank next lower than that which held her lovely form, with the dainty billows of lace and organdie rippling around me, and her little toes pressed into the small of my back. Was this a common, vulgar circus—with a menagerie attachment? To me it was the seventh heaven. The clown leaped lightly into the ring, cracked his whip, and began his witticisms. I heard him as one hears the murmur of the sea in his dreams. The beautiful bare-back rider galloped, ran, jumped, smiled, kissed her hand, and trotted off the stage with Master Clown at her heels and the whole scene was to me only as a scene in a painting on which my eye casually fell. The only living, breathing fact of which I was really conscious was that those blue eyes were shining like stars just over my head.

In the pauses of the drama, the lemonade man went by. What was he to me, or I to him? Noisy boys or verdant farming youths might patronize him at their will—I slaked my thirst with deep draughts of a nectar no lemonade-fellow could dispense at two cents a glass. While the cannon-ball man was catching a ten-pound ball between his teeth, and the boneless boy was tying himself in a double bow-knot, I was pleasing myself with images of the darling little Spitz I would seek, purchase, and present to Miss Flora in place of the one who had thoughtlessly swallowed my fish-hook.

"Were you ever in love, young man?" suddenly asked the clown, after the india-rubber athlete had got tired of turning himself, like a dozen flap-jacks on a hot griddle.

The question startled me. I looked up. It seemed to me, as he eyed me, that he had addressed it particularly to me. I blushed. Some strange country girls on either side of me began to titter. I blushed more decidedly. The motley chap in the ring must have seen it. He grinned from ear to ear, walked up to the very edge of the rope, and repeated:

"Were you ever in love, young man?"

There were young men all round me; he might have looked at Knickerbocker, or any one of a dozen others; if I had not been supersensitive I never should have imagined that he meant to be personal.

If I had not retained the self-possession of an egotist, I should have reflected that it was not the thing to notice the vulgar wit of a circus-clown. Unfortunately self-possession is the last possession of a bashful man. I half rose from my seat, demanding fiercely:

"Are you speaking to me, sir?"

"If the shoe fits, you can wear it," was the grinning answer; and then there was a shout from the whole audience—hooting, laughter, clapping of hands—and I felt that I had made a Dundreary of myself.

"We beg parding," went on the rascal, stepping back and bowing. "We had no intentions of being personal—meant no young gentleman in partikilar. We *always* make a point of asking a few questions in general. Here comes mademoiselle, the celebrated tight-rope dancer," etc., etc., and the thousand eyes which had been glued to my scarlet face were diverted to a new attraction.

"I'll thrash that scoundrel within an inch of his life," I said to young Knickerbocker, who was sitting behind me beside his sister.

"You will have to whip the whole circus, then; these fellows all stand by each other. Your policy is to let the matter drop."

"I'll whip the whole circus, then," I retorted, savagely.

"Please don't," said a soft voice, and I wilted under it.

"It maddens me to be always made ridiculous before *you*," I whispered. "I'm a dreadfully unfortunate man, Miss Knick——"

"*Fire!*"

A frightful cry in such a place as that! Something flashed up brightly—I saw flames about something in the ring—the crowd arose from the benches—women screamed—men yelled.

"Sit still, Flora!" I heard young Knickerbocker say, sternly.

I thought of a million things in the thousandth part of a second—of the flaming canvas, the deadly crush, the wild beasts, terrified and breaking from their cages. It was folly, it was madness, to linger a moment in hopes of the fire being subdued. I looked toward the entrance—it was not far from us; a few people were going quickly out. I was stronger than her brother; I could fight my way through any crowd with that slight form held in one arm.

"*Fire!*"

I dallied with fate no longer. Grasping Flora by her slender waist, I dragged her from her seat, and hurried her along through the thickening throng. When she could no longer keep her feet. I supported her entirely, elbowing, pushing, struggling with the maddest of them. I reached the narrow exit—I fought my way through like a tiger. Bleeding, exhausted, my hat gone, my coat torn from my back, I at last emerged under the calm moonlight with my darling held to my panting heart. Bearing her apart from the jostling crowd, I looked backward, expecting to see the devouring flames stream high from the combustible roof. As yet they had not broken through. I set my treasure gently down on her little feet. Her bonnet was gone, her wealth of golden hair hung disheveled about her pale face.

"Are we safe?" she murmured.

"Yes, thank Heaven, your precious life is saved!"

"Oh! where is my brother?"

"Here!" said a cold voice behind us, and young Knickerbocker coolly took his sister on his own arm. "What in the name of folly did you drag her off in that style for? A pretty-looking girl you are, Flora, I must say!"

"But the fire!" I gasped.

"Was all out in less than a minute. A lamp exploded, but fortunately set fire to nothing else. I never saw anything more utterly ridiculous than you dragging my sister off through that crowd, and me sitting still and laughing at you. I don't know whether to look on you as a hero or a fool, Mr. Flutter."

"Look on me as a blunderer," I said meekly.

But the revulsion of feeling was too great; I felt myself turning sick and faint, and when I knew anything again I was home in bed. And now I owe Miss Flora a new bonnet as well as a little dog.

CHAPTER XII.

A LEAP FOR LIFE.

It is impossible to make an ordinary person understand the chaos of mingled feelings with which I heard, two days after the circus performance in which I had so large a share, that Blue-Eyes and Company had departed for a tour of the watering-places—feelings of anguish and relief mixed in about equal proportions. I madly loved her, but I had known from the first that my love was hopeless, and the thought of meeting her, after having made myself so ridiculous, was torture. Therefore I felt relief that I was no longer in danger of encountering the mocking laughter of those blue eyes, but I lost my appetite. I moped, pined, grew pale, freckled, and listless.

"What's the use of wasting harvest apples making dumplings, when you don't eat none, John?" asked my aunt, one day at dinner, after the hands had left the table.

"Aunt," replied I, solemnly, "don't mock me with apple dumplings; they may be light, but my heart is heavy."

"La, John, try a little east on your heart," said she, laughing—by "east" she meant yeast, I suppose.

"No, aunt, not 'east,' but west. My mind is made up. I'm going out to Colorado to fight the Indians."

She let the two-tined steel fork drop out of her hand.

"What will your ma say to that?" she gasped.

"I tell you I am going," was my firm reply, and I went.

Yes, I had long sighed to be a Juan Fernandez, or a Mount Washington weatherologist, or something lonesome and sad, as my readers know. Fighting Indians would be a terrible risky business; but compared to facing the "girls of the period" it would be the merest play. I was weary of a life that was all mistakes. "Better throw it away," I thought, bitterly, "and give my scalp to dangle at a redskin's belt, than make another one of my characteristic and preposterous blunders."

I had heard that Buffalo Bill was about to start for the Rocky Mountains, and I wrote to New York asking permission to join him. He answered that I could, if I was prepared to pay my own way. I immediately bade my relatives farewell, went home, borrowed two hundred dollars of father, told mother she was the only woman I wasn't afraid of, kissed her good-bye, and met Buffalo Bill at the next large town by appointment, he being already on his way West. I came home *after dark*, and left again *before daylight*, and that was the last I saw of my native village for some time.

"You don't let on yer much of a fighter?" asked the great scout, as he saw me hunt all over six pockets and blush like a girl when the conductor came for our tickets, and finally hand him a postal-card instead of the bit of pasteboard he was impatiently waiting to punch.

"Oh, I guess I'll fight like a rat when it comes to that," I answered. "I'm brave as a lion—only I'm bashful."

"Great tomahawks! is that yer disease?" groaned Bill.

"Yes, that's my trouble," I said, quite confidentially, for somehow I seemed to get on with the brave hunter more easily than with the starched minions of society. "I'm bashful, and I'm tired of civilized life. I'm always putting my foot in it when I'm trying the hardest to keep it out. Besides, I'm in love, and the girl I want don't want me. It's either deliberate suicide or death on the plains with me."

"Precisely. I understand. *I've been thar!*" said Buffalo Bill; and we got along well together from the first.

He encouraged the idea that in my present state of mind I would make a magnificent addition to his chosen band; but I have since had some reason to believe that he was leading me on for the sole purpose of making a scarecrow of me—setting me up in some spot frequented by the redskins, to become their target, while he and his comrades scooped down from some ambush and wiped out a score or two of them after I had perished at my post. I *suspect* this was his plan. He probably considered that so stupid a blunderer as I deserved no better fate than to be used as a decoy. I think so myself. I have nothing like the extravagant opinion of my own merits that I had when I first launched out into the sea of human conflict.

At all events, Buffalo Bill was very kind to me all the way out to the plains; he protected me as if I had been a timid young lady—took charge of my tickets, escorted me to and fro from the station eating-houses, almost cut up my food and eating it for me; and if a woman did but glance in my direction, he scowled ferociously. Under such patronage I got through without any accident.

It was the last day of our ride by rail. In the car which we helped to occupy there was not a single female, and I was happy. A sense of repose—of safety—stole over me, which even the knowledge that on the morrow we were to take the war-path could not overcome.

"Oh," sighed I, "no women! This *is* bliss!"

In about five minutes after I had made this remark the train drew up at one of those little stations that mark off the road, and the scout got off a minute to see a man. Fatal minute! In that brief sixty seconds of time a female made her appearance in the car door, looked all along the line, and, either because the seat beside me was the only vacant one, or because she liked my looks, she came, and, without so much as "by your leave," plumped down by me.

"This seat is engaged," I mildly remonstrated, growing as usual very red.

She looked around at me, saw me blush, and began to titter.

"No, young man," said she, "I ain't engaged, but I told ma I bet I would be before I got to Californy."

By this time my protector had returned; but, seeing a woman, and a young woman at that, in his seat, he coolly ignored my imploring looks and passed out into the next car.

"I'm going on the platform to smoke," he whispered.

"Be *you* engaged?" continued my new companion.

"No, miss," I stammered.

"Ain't that lucky?" she giggled. "Who knows but what we may make up our minds to hitch horses afore we get to Californy!" and she eyed me all over without a bit of bashfulness, and seemed to admire me. My goodness! this was worse than Alvira Slimmens!

"But I'm only going a few hours farther, and I'm not a marrying man, and I'm bound for the Indian country," I murmured.

She remained silent a few moments, and I stole a side-glance at her. She was a sharp-looking girl; her hair was cut short, and in the morocco belt about her waist I saw the glitter of a small revolver. Before I had finished these observations she turned suddenly toward me, and her black eyes rested fully on me as she asked:

"Stranger, do you believe in love at first sight?"

"No—no, indeed, miss; not for worlds!" I murmured, startled.

"Well, I *do*," said she; "and mebbe you will, yet."

"I—I don't believe in anything of the kind," I reiterated, getting as far as possible into my corner of the seat.

"La! you needn't be bashful," she went on, laughing; "I ain't a-going to scourge you. Thar's room enough for both of us."

She subsided again, and again broke out:

"Bound for the Injun country, are you? So'm I. Whar do you get off?"

"I thought you said you were going to California?" I remarked, more and more alarmed.

Then that girl with the revolver winked at me slyly.

"I *am* going there—in the course of time; but I'm going by easy stages. I ain't in no hurry. I told ma I'd be married by the time I got there, and I mean to keep my word I may be six months going, yer see."

Another silence, during which I mutely wondered how long it would take Buffalo Bill to smoke his pipe.

"Don't believe in love at first sight! Sho!" resumed my companion. "You ain't got much spunk, you ain't! Why, last week a girl and a fellow got acquainted in this very car—this very seat, for all I know—and afore they reached Lone Tree Station they was *engaged*. There happened to be a clergyman going out to San Francisco on the train, and he married 'em afore sunset, he did. When I heerd of that, I said to myself, 'Sally Spitfire, why don't *you* fix up and travel, too? Who knows what may happen?'"

Unmerciful fates! had I fled from civilization only to fall a prey to a female like this? It looked like it. There wasn't much fooling about this damsel's love-making. Cold chills ran down my spine. My eye avoided hers; I bit my nails and looked out of the window.

"Ain't much of a talker, are ye?" she ran on. "That just suits me. My tongue is long enough for both of us. I always told ma I wouldn't marry a great talker—there'd be one too many in the house."

I groaned in anguish of spirit; I longed to see a thousand wild and painted warriors swoop down upon the train. I thought of our peaceful dry-goods store at home, and I would gladly have sat down in another butter-tub could I have been there. I even thought of earthquakes with a sudden longing; but we were not near enough the Western shore to hope for anything so good as an earthquake.

"I do wonder if thar's a clergyman on *this* train," remarked the young lady, reflectively.

"Supposing there is," I burst out, in desperation, "does any one need his services? Is anybody going to die?"

"Not as I know of," was the meaning reply, while Miss Spitfire looked at me firmly, placing her hand on her revolver as she spoke; "not if people behave as they ought—like gentlemen—and don't go trifling with an unprotected girl's affections in a railroad car."

"Who—who—who's been doing so?" I stammered.

"*You* have, and I hold you accountable. You've got to marry me. I've made up my mind. And when Sally Spitfire makes up her mind, she means it. To refuse my hand is to insult me, and no man shall insult me with safety. No, sir! not so long as I carry a Colt's revolver. I took a fancy to you, young man, the minute my eyes rested on you. I froze to you to oncst. I calculate to marry you right off. Will you inquire around for a clergyman? or shall I do it myself?"

"I will go," I said, quickly.

"P'raps I'd better go 'long," she said, suspiciously, and as I arose she followed suit, and we walked down the car together, she twice asking in a loud voice if there was a minister on board.

"One in the next car," at last spoke a fellow, looking at us with a broad grin.

We stepped out on the platform to enter the next car—now was my time—now or never! I looked at the ground—it was tolerably level and covered with grass; the train was running at moderate speed; there was but one way to escape my tormentor. Making my calculations as accurately as possible, I suddenly leaped from the steps of the car; my head and feet seemed driven into one another; I rolled over and over—thought I was dead, was surprised to find I was not dead, picked myself up, shook myself.

"Ha! ha! ha!" I laughed hysterically; "I'm out of that scrape, anyway!"

"Oh, are you?" said a voice behind me.

I whirled about. As true as I'm writing this, there stood that girl! Her hat was knocked off, her nose was bleeding, but she was smiling right in my face.

I cast a look of anguish at the retreating train. No one had noticed our mad leap; and the cars were gliding smoothly away—away—leaving me alone on the wide plains with that determined female!

CHAPTER XIII.

ONE OF THE FAIR SEX COMES TO HIS RESCUE.

Before I comprehended that the indomitable female stood beside me, the train was puffing pitilessly away.

"Oh, stop! stop! stop! stop!" I called and yelled in an agony of apprehension; but I might as well have appealed to the wind that went whistling by.

"Perhaps the locomotive will hear you, and down brakes of its own accord," said Miss Spitfire, scornfully. "I told ma I was gwine to get a husband 'fore I got to Californy, an' I *have* got one. You jest set down on that bowlder, an' don't you try to make a move till the train from 'Frisco comes along. Then you git aboard along with me, an' if there ain't no minister to be found in them cars, I'll haul you off at Columbus, where there's two to my certain knowledge."

She had her revolver in her hand, directed *point blank* at my quivering, quaking heart. Though I am bashful, I am no coward, and I thought for full two minutes that I'd let her fire away, if such was her intention.

"Better be dead than live in a land so full of women that I can never hope for any comfort!" I thought, bitterly; and so confronted the enemy in the growing calmness of despair.

"Ain't you a-going fur to set down on that bowlder?"

"No, madam, I am *not*! I would rather be shot than married, at any time. Why! I was going to fight the Indians with Buffalo Bill, on purpose to get rid of the girls."

Sally looked at me curiously; her outstretched arm settled a little until the revolver pointed at my knee instead of my heart.

"P'raps you've been disappointed in love?" she queried.

"Not that entirely," I answered, honestly.

"P'raps you've run away from a breach of promise?"

"Oh, no! no, indeed!"

"What on airth do you want to get rid o' the girls fur, then?"

"Miss Spitfire," said I, scraping the gravel with the toe of my boot, "I'm afraid of them. I'm bashful."

"BASHFUL!" Miss Spitfire cried, and then she began to laugh.

She laughed and laughed until I believed and hoped she would laugh herself into pieces. The idea struck this creature in so ludicrous a light that she nearly went into convulsions. *She*, alas, had never been troubled by such a weakness. I watched my opportunity, when she was doubled up with mirth, to snatch the revolver from her hand.

The tables were now turned, but not for long. She sprang at me like a wildcat; I defended myself as well as I could without really hurting her, maintaining my hold on the revolver, but not attempting to use it on my scratching, clawing antagonist. The station-master came out of Lone Tree station, a mile away, and walked up the track to see what was going on. Of course he had no notion of what it was, but it amused him to see the fight, and he kept cheering and urging on Miss Sally, probably with the idea that she was my wife and we were indulging in a domestic squabble. At the same time it chanced that a boat load of six or eight of the roughest fellows it had ever been my lot to meet, and all with their belts stuck full of knives and revolvers, came rowing across the river, not far away, and landed just in time to "see the fun." When Miss Spitfire saw these ruffians she ceased clawing and biting me, and appealed to them.

I was dumbfounded by the falsehood ready on her lips.

"Will you, *gentlemen*," said she, "stand by and see a young lady deserted by this sneak?"

"What's up?" asked a brawny fellow, seven feet high, glaring at me as if he thought I had committed seventeen murders.

"I'll tell you," responded Spitfire, panting for breath. "We was engaged to be married, we was, all fair an' square. He pretended to be goin' through the train to look fur a minister fur to tie the knot, an' just sneaked off the train, when it stopped yere; but I see him in time, an' I jumped off, too, an' I nabbed him."

"Shall we hang the little skunk up to yonder tree? or shall we set him up fur a target an' practice firing at a mark fur about five minutes? Will do whatever you say, young lady. We're a rough set; but we don't lay out to see no wimmen treated scurvy."

I'm no coward, as I said, but I dare say my face was not very smiling as I met the flashing eyes and saw the scowling brows of those giant ruffians, whose hands were already drawing the bowie-knives and pistols from their belts. But I steadied my voice and spoke up:

"Boys," said I, very friendly, "what's the use of a pair hitching together who do not like each other, and who will always be uneasy in harness? If I married her, she would be sorry. Come, let us go up to the station and have something to drink. Choose your own refreshments, and don't be backward."

There was a good deal of growling and muttering; but the temptation was irresistible. The result was that in half an hour not a drop of liquor remained to the poor fellow who kept the station— that I paid up the score "like a man," as my drunken companions assured me, who now clapped me familiarly on the shoulder, and called me "Little Grit," as a pet name—that Miss Spitfire, minus her revolver, sat biting her nails about two rods away—and that she waited anxiously for the expected arrival of the 'Frisco train, bound eastward.

"Come, now, Little Grit," said the leader of the band, when the whisky had all disappeared, "you was gwine with Buffalo Bill; better come along with me—I'm a better fellow, an' hev killed more Injuns than ever Bill did. We're arter them pesky redskins now. A lot of 'em crossed the stream a couple o' nights ago, and stole our best horses. We're bound to hev 'em back. Some o' them red thieves will miss their skalps afore to-morrow night. A feller as kin fight a woman is jist the chap for us. You come along; we'll show you how to tree your first Injun."

The long and the short of it was I had to go. I did not want to. I thought of my mother, of Belle, of Blue-Eyes, and I hung back. But I was taken along. These giants, with their bristling belts, did not understand a person who said "no" to them. And as the secondary effect of the liquor was to make them quarrelsome, I had to pretend that I liked the expedition.

Not to weary the reader, we tracked the marauders, and came across them at earliest dawn the following morning, cooking their dog-stew under the shelter of a high bluff, with the stolen horses picketed near, in a cluster of young cottonwoods.

I have no talent for depicting skirmishes with the redskins; I leave all that to Buffalo Bill. I will here simply explain that the Indians were surprised, but savage; that the whites were resolved to get back their horses, and that they did get them, and rode off victorious, leaving six dead and nine wounded red warriors on the battle-ground, with only one mishap to their own numbers.

The mishap was a trifling one to the border ruffians. It was not so trifling to me.

It consisted of their leaving me a prisoner in the hands of the Indians.

I was bound to a tree, while the wretches jabbered around me, as to what they should do for me. Then, while I was reflecting whether I would not prefer marriage with Miss Spitfire to this horrible predicament, they drove a stake into the ground, untied me, led me to the stake, re-tied me to that, and piled branches of dry cottonwood about me up to my neck.

Then one of them ran, howling, to bring a brand from the fire under the upset breakfast pot.

I raised my eyes to the bright sun, which had risen over the plain, and was smiling at my despair. The hideous wretch came running with the fire-brand. The braves leaped, danced, and whooped.

I closed my eyes. Then a sharp, shrill yell pierced the air, and in another moment something touched my neck. It was not the scorching flames I dreaded. I opened my eyes. A hideous face, copper-colored, distorted by a loving grin, was close to mine; a pair of arms were about my neck—a pair of woman's arms! They were those of a ferocious and ugly squaw, old enough to be my mother. The warrior with the fire-brand was replacing it, with a disappointed expression, under the stewed dog. *I was saved!*

All in a flash I comprehended the truth. Here was I, John Flutter, enacting the historical part of the John Smith, of Virginia, who was rescued by the lovely Pocahontas.

This hideous creature smirking in my face was my Pocahontas. It was not leap-year, but she had chosen me for her brave. The charms of civilized life could no longer trouble me. She would lovingly paint my face, hang the wampum about my waist, and lead me to her wigwam in the wilderness, where she would faithfully grind my corn and fricassee my puppy. It was for *this* I had escaped Sally Spitfire—for *this* that my unhappy bashfulness had driven me far from home and friends.

She unfastened the rope from the stake, and led me proudly away. My very soul blushed with shame. Oh, fatal, fatal blunder!

CHAPTER XIV.

HIS DIFFIDENCE BRINGS ABOUT AN ACCIDENT.

That was a long day for me. I could not eat the dog-bone which my Pocahontas handed me, having drawn it from the kettle with her own sweet fingers. We traveled all day; having lost their stolen horses as well as their own ponies, the savages had to foot it back to their tribe. I could see that they got as far away from the railroad and from traces of white men as possible.

It began to grow dark, and we were still plodding along. I was foot-sore, discouraged, and woe-begone. All the former trials of my life, which had seemed at the time so hard to bear, now appeared like the merest trifles.

Ah, if I were only home again! How gladly would I sit down in butter-tubs, and spill hot tea into my lap! How joyfully would I walk up the church aisles, with my ears burning, and sit down on my new beaver in father's pew of a Sunday. How sweet would be the suppressed giggle of the saucy girls behind me! How easily, how almost audaciously, would I ask Miss Miller if I might see her home! What an active part I would take in debating societies! Vain dream! My hideous Pocahontas marched stolidly on, dragging me like a frightened calf, at the rope's end. My throat was dry as ashes. I guess the redskins suffered for want of water, too. We came to a little brackish stream after sunset, and here they camped. They had taken from me Miss Spitfire's revolver, or I should have shot myself.

The squaws made some suppawn in a big kettle, and my squaw brought me some in a dirty wooden bowl. I was too homesick to eat, and this troubled her. She tried to coax me, with atrocious grins and nods, to eat the smoking suppawn. I couldn't, and she looked unhappy.

Then something happened—something hit the bowl and sent the hot mush flying into my beauty's face, and spattering over me. At the

80

same instant about twenty Indians were hit, also, and went tumbling over, with their mouths full of supper. There were yells, and jumps, and a general row. I jerked away from Pocahontas and ran as fast as my tired legs would carry me. I went toward the attacking party. It might be of Indians too, but I didn't care. I was afraid of Pocahontas—more afraid of her than of any braves in the world. But these invaders proved to be white men; a large party of miners going toward Pike's Peak, by wagon instead of by the new railroad.

I threw myself on their protection. They had routed out the savages, and now took possession of their camping-ground. I passed a peaceful night; except that my dreams were disturbed by visions of Pocahontas. In the morning my new friends proposed that I should join their party, and try my luck in the mining regions; they were positive that each would find more gold than he knew what to do with.

"Then you can go home and marry some pretty girl, my boy," said one friendly fellow, slapping me on the shoulder.

"Never," I murmured. "I have no object in life, save one."

"And what is that, my young friend?"

"To go where there never has been nor never will be a woman."

"Good! the mines will be just the place then. None of the fair sex there, my boy. You can enjoy the privilege of doing up your own linen to the fullest extent. You won't have anybody to iron your collars there, you bet."

"Lead on—I follow!" I cried, almost like an actor on the stage.

I felt exhilarated—a wild, joyous sense of freedom. My two recent narrow escapes added to the pleasure with which I viewed my present prospects. This was better than sailing for some Juan Fernandez, or being clerk of the weather on Mount Washington. Ho! for Pike's Peak. In those high solitudes, while heaping up the yellow gold which should purchase all the luxuries of life for the woman whom *sometime* I should choose, I could, at the same time, be gradually overcoming my one weakness. When I did see fit to return to my native village, no man should be so calm, so cool, so self-possessed as John Flutter, Jr., mine-owner, late of the Rocky Mountains. I felt very bold over the prospect. I was not a bit bashful just then. I joined the adventurers, paying them in money for my seat in their wagons, and my place at their camp-table. In due time we reached the scene of action. I would not go into any of the canvas villages which had sprung up like mushrooms. There might be a woman in some one of these places. I went directly into the hills, where I bought out a sick man's claim, and went to work. I blistered my white hands, but I didn't mind that much—there were no blue eyes to notice the disfigurement.

I had been at work six days. I was a good young man, and I would not dig on Sunday, as some of the fellows did. I sat in the door of my little hut, and read an old newspaper, and thought of those far-away days when I used to be afraid of the girls. How glad I felt that I was outgrowing that folly. A shadow fell across my paper, and I glanced up. Thunder out of a clear sky could not so have astonished me. There stood a young lady, smiling at me! None of those rough Western pioneer girls, either, but a pale, delicate, beautiful young lady, about eighteen, with cheeks like wild roses, so faintly, softly flushed with the fatigue of climbing, and great starry hazel eyes, and dressed in a fashionable traveling suit, made up in the latest style.

"Pardon me, sir, for startling you so," she said, pleasantly. "Can you give me a drink of water? I have been climbing until I am thirsty. Papa is not far behind, around the rock there. I out-climbed him, you see—as I told him I could!" and she laughed like an angel.

Yes! it was splendid to find how I had improved! I jumped to my feet and made a low bow. I wasn't red in the face—I wasn't confused—I didn't stammer; I felt as cool as I do this moment, as I answered her courteously:

"Cer-cer-certainly, madam—miss, I mean—you shall have a spring fresh from me—a drink, I mean—we've a nice, cold spring in the rocks just behind the cabin; I'll get you one in a second."

"No such *great* hurry, sir"—another smile.

I dashed inside and brought a tin cup—my only goblet—hurried to the spring, and brought her the sparkling draught, saying, as I handed it to her:

"You must excuse the din tipper, miss."

She took it politely! and began to quaff, but from some reason she choked and choked, and finally shook so, that she spilled the water all over the front breadth of her gray-check silk. She was laughing at my "din tipper," just as if the calmest people did not sometimes get the first letters of their words mixed up.

While she giggled and pretended to cough the old gentleman came in sight, puffing and blowing like a porpoise, and looking very warm. He told me he was "doing the mountains" for his daughter's health, and that they were going on to California to spend the winter; ending by stating that he was thirsty too, and so fatigued with his climb that he would be obliged to me if I would add a stick in his, if I had it. Now I kept a little whisky for medicine, and I was only too anxious to oblige the girl's father, so I darted into the cabin again and brought out one of the two bottles which I owned—two bottles, just alike, one containing whisky, the other kerosene. In my confusion I—well, I was very hospitable, and I added as much kerosene as there was water; and when he had taken three large swallows, he began to spit and splutter; then to groan; then to double up on the hard rock in awful convulsions. I smelled the kerosene, and I felt that I had murdered him. It had come to this at last! My bashfulness was to do worse than urge me to suicide—it was to be the means of my causing the death of an estimable old gentleman—her father! She began to cry and wring her hands. As yet she did not suspect me! She supposed her father had fallen in a fit of apoplexy.

"If he dies, I will allow her always to think so," I resolved.

My eyes stuck out of my head with terror at what I had done. I was rooted to the ground. But only for a moment. Remorse, for once, made me self-possessed. I remembered that I had salt in the cabin. I got some, mixed it with water, and poured it down his throat. It had the desired effect, soon relieving him of the poisonous dose he had swallowed.

"Ah! you have saved my papa's life!" cried the young lady, pressing my trembling hand.

"Saved it!" growled old Cresus, as he sat up and glared about. "Let him alone, Imogen! He tried to poison and murder me, so as to rob me after I was dead, and keep you prisoner, my pet. The scoundrel!"

"It was all a mistake—a wretched mistake!" I murmured.

He wouldn't believe me; but he was too ill to get up, as he wanted. I tried to make him more comfortable by assisting him to a seat on my keg of blasting powder.

As he began to revive a little, he drew a cigar from his pocket, and asked me if I had a match. I had none; but there was a small fire under my frying-pan, and I brought him a coal on a chip. Miss Imogen, when she saw the coal on the chip, began to laugh again. That embarrassed me. My nerves were already unstrung, and my trembling fingers unfortunately spilled the burning ember just as the old gentleman was about to stoop over it with his cigar. It fell between his knees, onto the head of the keg, rolled over, and dropped plumb through the bung-hole onto the giant-powder inside.

This cured me of my bashfulness for some time, as it was over a week before I came to my senses.

CHAPTER XV.

HE BECOMES ACQUAINTED WITH A CHICAGO WIDOW.

I came to my senses in one of the bedrooms of the Shantytown Hotel. There was only a partition between that and the other bedrooms of brown cotton cloth, and as I slowly became conscious of things about me, I heard two voices beyond the next curtain talking of my affairs.

"I reckon he won't know where the time's gone to when he comes to himself ag'in. Lucky for him he didn't go up, like the old gentleman, in such small pieces as to never come down. I don't see, fur the life of me, what purvented. He was standin' right over the kag on which the old chap sot. Marakalous escape, that of the young lady. Beats everything."

"You bet, pardner, 'twouldn't happen so once in a thousand times. You see, she was jist blowed over the ledge an' rolled down twenty or thirty feet, an' brought up on a soft spot—wa'n't hurt a particle. But how she does take on about her pop! S'pose you knew her brother's come on fur her?"

"No."

"Yes; got here by the noon stage. They're reckoning to leave Shantytown immegitly. Less go down and see 'em off!"

They shuffled away.

I don't know whether my head ached, but I know my heart did. I was a murderer. Or, if not quite so bad as a deliberate murderer, I was, at the very least, guilty of manslaughter. And why? Because I had not been able to overcome my wicked weakness. I felt sick of life, of everything—especially of the mines.

"I can never return to the scene of the accident," I thought.

I groaned and tossed, but it was the torture of my conscience, and not of my aching limbs. The doctor and others came in.

"How long shall I have to lie here?" I asked.

"Not many days; no bones are broken. Your head is injured and you are badly bruised, that's all. You must keep quiet—you must not excite yourself."

Excite myself! As if I could, for one moment, forget the respectable old capitalist whom I had first poisoned and then blown into ten thousand pieces through my folly. I had brain fever. It set in that night. For two weeks I raved deliriously; for two weeks I was doing the things I ought not to have done—in imagination. I took a young lady skating, and slipped down with her on the ice, and broke her Grecian nose. I went to a grand reception, and tore the point lace flounce off of Mrs. Grant's train, put my handkerchief in my saucer, and my coffee-cup in my pocket. I was left to entertain a handsome young lady, and all I could say was to cough and "Hem! hem!" until at last she asked me if I had any particular article I would like hemmed.

I killed a baby by sitting down on it in a fit of embarrassment, when asked by a neighbor to take a seat. I waltzed and waltzed and waltzed with Blue-Eyes, and every time I turned I stepped on her toes with my heavy boots, until they must have been jelly in her little satin slippers, and finally we fell down-stairs, and I went out of that fevered dream only to find myself again giving blazing kerosene to an estimable old gentleman, who swallowed it unsuspiciously, and then sat down on a powder keg, and we all blew up—up—up—and came down—down—bump! I never want to have brain fever again—at least, not until I have conquered myself.

When I was once more rational, I resolved that a miner's life was too rough for me; and, as soon as I could be bolstered up in a corner of the coach, I set out to reach the railroad, where I was to take a palace-car for home. I gained strength rapidly during the change and excitement of the journey; so that, the day before we were to reach Chicago, I no longer remained prone in my berth, but, "clothed and in my right mind," took my seat with the other passengers, looked about and tried to forget the past and to enjoy myself. At first, I had a seat to myself; but, at one of the stations, about two in the afternoon, a lady, dressed in deep black, and wearing a heavy crepe veil, which concealed her face, entered our car, and slipped quietly in to the vacant half of my seat. She sat quite motionless, with her veil down. Every few moments a long, tremulous, heart-broken sigh stirred this sable curtain which shut in my companion's face. I felt a deep sympathy for her, whoever she might be, old or young, pretty or ugly. I inferred that she was a widow; I could hear that she was in affliction; but I was far too diffident to invent any little courteous way of expressing my sympathy. In about half an hour, she put her veil to one side, and asked me, in a low, sweet, pathetic voice, if I had any objection to drawing down the blind, as her veil smothered her, and she had wept so much that her eyes could not bear the strong light of the afternoon sun. I drew down the blind—with such haste as to pinch my fingers cruelly between the sash and the sill.

"Oh, I am *so* sorry!" said she.

"It's of no consequence," I stammered, making a Toots of myself.

"Oh, but *it is*! and in my service too! Let me be your surgeon, sir," and she took from her traveling-bag a small bottle of cologne, with which she drenched a delicate film of black-bordered handkerchief, and then wound the same around my aching fingers. "You are pale," she continued, slightly pressing my hand before releasing it—"ah, how sorry I am!"

"I am pale because I have been ill recently," I responded, conscious that all my becoming pallor was changing to turkey-red.

"Ill?—oh, how sad! What a world of trouble we live in! Ill?—and so young—so hand——. Excuse me, I meant not to flatter you, but I have seen so much sorrow myself. I am only twenty-two, and I've been a wid—wid—wid—ow over a year."

She wiped away a tear with handkerchief No. 2, and smiled sadly in my face.

"Sorrow has aged her," I thought, for, although the blind was down, she looked to me nearer thirty than twenty-two.

Still, she was pretty, with dark eyes that looked into yours in a wonderfully confiding way—melting, liquid, deep eyes, that even a man who is perfectly self-possessed can not see to the bottom of soon enough for his own good. As for me, those eyes confused while they pleased me. The widow never noticed my embarrassment; but, the ice once broken, talked on and on. She gave me, in soft, sweet, broken accents, her history—how she had been her mother's only pet, and had married a rich Chicago broker, who had died in less than two years, leaving her alone—all alone—with plenty of money, plenty of jewelry, a fine house, but alas, "no one to love her, none to caress," as the song says, and the world a desert.

"But I can still love *a friend*," she added, with a melancholy smile. "One as disinterested, as ignorant of the world as you, would please me best. You must stop in Chicago," she said, giving me her card before we parted. "Every traveler should spend a few days in our wonderful city. Call on me, and I will have up my carriage and take you out to see the sights."

Need I say that I stopped in Chicago? or add that I went to call on the fair widow? She took me out driving according to promise. I found that she was just the style of woman that suited me best. I was bashful; she was not. I was silent; she could keep up the conversation with very little aid from me. With such a woman as that I could get along in life. She would always be willing to take the lead. All I would have to do would be to give her the reins, and she would keep the team going. She would be willing to walk the first into church—to interview the butcher and baker—to stand between me and the world. A wife like that would be some comfort to a bashful man. Besides, she was rich! Had she not said it? I have seldom had a happier hour than that of our swift, exhilarating drive. The colored driver, gorgeous in his handsome livery, kept his eyes and ears to himself. I lolled back in the luxurious carriage beside my charmer. I forgot the unhappy accident of the blasting-powder—all the mortifications and disappointments of my life. I reveled in bliss. For once, I had nothing to do but be courted. How often had I envied the girls their privilege of keeping quiet and being made love to. How often had I sighed to be one of the sex who is popped to and does not have to pop. And now, this lovely, brilliant creature who sat beside me, having been once married, and seeing my natural timidity, "knew how it was herself," and took on her own fair hands all the responsibility.

"Mr. Flutter," said she, "I know just how you feel—you want to ask me to marry you, but you are too bashful. Have I guessed right?"

I pressed her hand in speechless assent.

"Yes, my dear boy, I knew it. Well, this is leap-year, and I will not see you sacrificed to your own timidity. I am yours, whenever you wish—to-morrow if you say so—yours forever. You shall have no trouble about it, I will speak to the Rev. Mr. Coalyard myself—I know him. When shall it be?—speak, dearest!"

I gasped out "to-morrow," and buried my blushing face on her shoulder.

For a moment her soft arms were twined around me—a moment only, for we were on the open lake drive. Not more than ten seconds did the pretty widow embrace me, but that was time enough, as I learned to my sorrow, for her to extract my pocket-book, containing the five hundred dollars I still had remaining from the sale of my mining-stock, and not one dollar of which did I ever see again.

CHAPTER XVI.

AT LAST HE SECURES A TREASURE.

I had to pawn my watch to get away from Chicago, for the police failed to find my pretty widow. The thought of getting again under my mother's wing was as welcome as my desire to get away from it had been eager. At night my dreams were haunted by all sorts of horrible fire-works, where old gentlemen sat down on powder-kegs, etc. Oh, for home! I knew there were no widows in my native village, except Widow Green, and I was not afraid of her. Well, I took the cars once more, and I had been riding two days and a night, and was not over forty miles from my destination, when the little incident occurred which proved to lead me into one of the worst blunders of all. It's *awful* to be a bashful young man! Everybody takes advantage of you. You are the victim of practical jokes—folks laugh if you do nothing on earth but enter a room. If you happen to hit your foot against a stool, or trip over a rug, or call a lady "sir," the girls giggle and the boys nudge each other, as if it were extremely amusing. But to blow up a confiding Wall street speculator, and to be swindled out of all your money by a pretty widow, is enough to make a sensitive man a raving lunatic. I had all this to think of as I was whirled along toward home. So absorbed was I in melancholy reflection, that I did not notice what was going on until a sudden shrill squawk close in my ear caused me to turn, when I found that a very common-looking young woman, with a by no means interesting infant of six months, had taken the vacant half of my seat. I was annoyed. There were plenty of unoccupied seats in the car, and I saw no reason why she should intrude upon my comfort. The infant shrieked wildly when I looked at it; but its mother stopped its mouth with one of those what-do-you-call-'ems that are stuck on the end of a flat bottle containing sweetened milk, and, after sputtering and gurgling in a vain attempt to keep on squalling, it subsided and went vigorously to work. It seemed after a time to become more accustomed to my harmless visage, and stared at me stolidly, with round, unwinking eyes, after it had exhausted the contents of the bottle.

In about half an hour the train stopped at a certain station; the conductor yelled out "ten minutes for refreshments," the eating-house man rang a big bell, and the passengers, many of them, hurried out. Then the freckle-faced woman leaned toward me.

"Are you goin' out?" said she.

"No," I replied, politely; "I am not far from home, and prefer waiting for my lunch until I get there."

"WOULD YOU HOLD MY BABY WHILE I RUN IN AN' GET A CUP O' TEA?"

"Then," said she, very earnestly, "would you hold my baby while I run in an' get a cup o' tea? Indeed, sir, I'm half famished, riding over twenty-four hours, and only a biscuit or two in my bag, and I must get some milk for baby's bottle or she'll starve."

It was impossible, under such circumstances, for one to refuse, though I would have preferred to head a regiment going into battle, for there were three young ladies, about six seats behind me, who were eating their lunch in the car, and I knew they would laugh at me; besides, the woman gave me no chance to decline, for she thrust the wide-eyed terror into my awkward arms, and rushed quickly out to obtain her cup of tea.

Did you ever see a bashful young man hold a strange baby? I expect I furnished—I and the baby—a comic opera, music and all, for the entertainment of the three girls, as they nibbled their cold chicken and pound-cake. For the mother had not been gone over fifteen seconds when that confounded young one began to cry. I sat her down on my knee and trotted her. She screamed with indignation, and grew so purple in the face I thought she was strangling, and I patted her on the back. This liberty she resented by going into a sort of spasm, legs and arms flying in every direction, worse than a wind-mill in a gale.

"This will never do," I thought; at the same time I was positive I heard a suppressed giggle in my rear.

A happy thought occurred to me—infants were always tickled with watches! But, alas I had pawned mine. However, I had a gold locket in my pocket, with my picture in it, which I had bought in Chicago, to present to the widow, and didn't present: this I drew forth and dangled before the eyes of the little infernal threshing-machine.

The legs and arms quieted down; the fat hands grabbed the glittering trinket. "Goo—goo—goo—goo," said the baby, and thrust the locket in her mouth. I think she must have been going through the interesting process of teething, for she made so many dents in the handsome face, that it was rendered useless as a future gift to some fortunate girl, while the way she slobbered over it was disgusting. I scarcely regretted the ruin of the locket, I was so delighted to have her keep quiet; but, alas! the little wretch soon dropped it and began howling like ten thousand midnight cats. I trotted her again—I tossed her—I laid her over my knees on her stomach—I said "Ssh—ssh—ssssh—sssssh!" all in vain. Instead of ten minutes for refreshments it seemed to me that they gave ten hours.

In desperation I raised her and hung her over my shoulder, rising at the same time and walking up and down the aisle. The howling ceased: but now the young ladies, after choking with suppressed laughter, finally broke into a scream of delight. Something must be up! I took the baby down and looked over my shoulder—the little rip had opened her mouth and sent a stream of white, curdy milk down the back of my new overcoat. For one instant the fate of that child hung in the balance. I walked to the door, and made a movement to throw her to the dogs; but humanity gained the day, and I refrained.

I felt that my face was redder than the baby's; every passenger remaining in the car was smiling. I went calmly back, and laid her down on the seat, while I took off my coat and made an attempt to remove the odious matters with my handkerchief, which ended by my throwing the coat over the back of the seat in disgust, resolving that mother would have to finish the job with her "Renovator." My handkerchief I threw out of the window.

Thank goodness! the engine bell was ringing at last and the people crowding back into the train.

I drew a long breath of relief, snatched the shrieking infant up again, for fear the mother would blame me for neglecting her ugly brat — and waited.

"All aboard!" shouted the conductor; the bell ceased to ring, the wheels began to revolve, the train was in motion.

"Great Jupiter Ammen!" I thought, while a cold sweat started out all over me, "she will be left!"

The cars moved faster and more mercilessly fast; the conductor appeared at the door; I rose and rushed toward him, the baby in my arms, crying:

"For Heaven's sake, conductor, stop the cars!"

"What's up?" he asked.

"What's up? Stop the cars, I say! Back down to the station again! *This baby's mother's left!*"

"Then she left on purpose," he answered coolly; "she never went into the eating-house at all. I saw her making tall tracks for the train that goes the other way. I thought it was all right. I didn't notice she hadn't her baby with her. I'll telegraph at the next station; that's all that can be done now."

This capped the climax of all my previous blunders! Why had I blindly consented to care for that woman's progeny? Why? why? Here was I, John Flutter, a young, innocent, unmarried man, approaching the home of my childhood with an infant in my arms! The horror of my situation turned me red and pale by turns as if I had apoplexy or heart disease.

There was always a crowd of young people down at the depot of our village; what would they think to see me emerge from the cars carrying that baby? Even the child seemed astonished, ceasing to cry, and staring around upon the passengers as if in wonder and amazement at our predicament. Yet not one of those heartless travelers seemed to pity me; every mouth was stretched in a broad grin; not a woman came forward and offered to relieve me of my burden; and thus, in the midst of my embarrassment and horror, the train rolled up to the well-known station, and I saw my father and mother, and half the boys and girls of the village, crowding the platform and waiting to welcome my arrival.

CHAPTER XVII.

HE ENJOYS HIMSELF AT A BALL.

Once more I was settled quietly down to my old life, clerking in my father's store. You would naturally suppose that my travels would have given me some confidence, and that I had worn out, as it were, the bashfulness of youth; but in my case this was an inborn quality which I could no more get rid of, than I could of my liver or my spleen.

I had never confessed to any one the episode of the giant-powder or the Chicago widow; but the story of the baby had crept out, through the conductor, who told it to the station-master. If you want to know how *that* ended, I'll just tell you that, maddened by the grins and giggles of the passengers, I started for the car door with that baby, but, in passing those three giggling young ladies, I suddenly slung the infant into their collective laps, and darted out upon the station platform. That's the way I got out of that scrape.

As I was saying, after all those dreadful experiences, I was glad to settle down in the store, where I honestly strove to overcome my weakness; but it was still so troublesome that father always interfered when the girls came in to purchase dry-goods. He said I almost destroyed the profits of the business, giving extra measure on ribbons and silks, and getting confused over the calicoes. But I'm certain the shoe was on the other foot; there wasn't a girl in town would go anywhere else to shop when they could enjoy the fun of teasing me; so that if I made a few blunders, I also brought custom.

Cold weather came again, and I was one year older. There was a grand ball on the twenty-second of February, to which I invited Hetty Slocum, who accepted my escort. We expected to have lots of fun. The ball-room was in the third story of the Spread-Eagle Hotel. There was to be a splendid supper at midnight in the big dining-room; hot oysters "in every style," roast turkey, chicken-pie, coffee, and all the sweet fixings.

It turned out to be a clear night; I took Hetty to the hotel in father's fancy sleigh, in good style, and having got her safely to the door of the ladies' parlor without a blunder to mar my peace of mind, except that I stepped on her slippered foot in getting into the sleigh, and crushed it so, that Hetty could hardly dance for the pain, I began to feel an unusual degree of confidence in myself, which I fortified by a stern resolution, on no account to get to blushing and stammering, but to walk coolly up to the handsomest girls and ask them out on the floor with all the self-possessed gallantry of a man of the world.

Alas! "the best-laid plans of mice an' men must aft gang," like a balky horse—just opposite to what you want them to. I spoke to my acquaintances in the bar-room easily enough, but when one after one the fellows went up to the door of the ladies' dressing-room to escort their fair companions to the ball-room, I felt my courage oozing away, until, under the pretext of keeping warm by the fire, I remained in the bar-room until every one else had deserted it. Then I slowly made my way up, intending to enter the gentlemen's dressing-room, to tie my white cravat, and put on my white kids. I found the room deserted—every one had entered the ball-room but myself; I could hear the gay music of the violins, and the tapping of the feet on the floor overhead. Surely it was time that I had called for *my* lady, and taken her up.

I knew that Hetty would be mad, because I had made her lose the first dance; yet, I fooled and fooled over the tying of my cravat, dreading the ordeal of entering the ball-room with a lady on my arm. At last it was tied. I turned to put on my gloves; then, for the first time, I was made aware that I had mistaken the room. I was in the ladies', not the gentlemen's dressing-room. There were the heaps of folded cloaks, and shawls, and the hoods. That very instant, before I could beat a retreat, I heard voices at the door—Hetty's among them. I glared around for some means of escape. There were none. What excuse could I make for my singular intrusion? Would it be believed if I swore that I had been unaware of the character of my surroundings? Would I be suspected of being a kleptomaniac? In the intensity of my mortification I madly followed the first impulse which moved me. This was to dive under the bed.

I had no more than taken refuge in this curious hiding-place, than I regretted the foolish act; to be discovered there would be infamy and disgrace too deep for words. I would have crawled out at the last second, but it was too late; I heard the girls in the room, and was forced to try and keep still as a mouse, though my heart thumped so I was certain they must hear it.

"Where do you suppose he has gone?" asked one.

"Goodness knows," answered Hetty. "I have looked in the gentlemen's room—he's not there. Catch me going to a ball with John Flutter again."

"It's a real insult, his not coming for you," added another; "but, la! you must excuse it. I know what's the trouble. I'll bet you two cents he's afraid to come up-stairs. He! he! he!"

Then all of them tittered "he! he! he" and "ha! ha! ha!"

"Did you ever see such a bashful young fellow?"

"He's a perfect goose!"

"Isn't it fun alive to tease him?"

"Do you remember when he tumbled in the lake?"

"Oh! and the time he sat down in the butter-tub?"

"Yes; and that day he came to our house and sat down in Old Mother Smith's cap instead of a vacant chair, because he was blushing so it made him blind."

"Well, if he hadn't crushed my foot getting into the sleigh, I wouldn't care," added Hetty, spitefully. "I shall limp all the evening."

"I do despise a blundering, stupid fellow that can't half take care of a girl."

"Yes; but what would you do without Mr. Flutter to laugh at?"

"That's so. As long as he stays around we will have somebody to amuse us."

"He'd be good-looking if he wasn't always so red in the face."

"If I was in his place I'd never go out without a veil."

"To hide his blushes?"

"Of course. What a pity he forgot to take his hat off in church last Sunday, until his mother nudged him."

"Yes. Did you hear it smash when he put his foot in it when he got up to go?"

Heavens and earth! There I was, under the bed, an enforced listener to this flattering conversation. My breast nearly burst with anger at them, at myself, at a cruel fate which had sent me into the world, doomed to grow up a bashful man. If, by falling one thousand feet plumb down, I could have sunk through that floor, I would have run the risk.

"You heard about the ba— —" began Hetty.

It was too much! In my torment I moved my feet without meaning to, and they hit against the leg of the bedstead with some force.

"What's that?"

"A cat under the bed, I should say."

"More likely a rat. Oh, girls! it may gnaw our cloaks; mine is under there, I know."

"Well, let us drive it out."

"Oh! oh! oh! I'm afraid!"

"I'm not; I'm going to see what is under there."

My heart ceased to beat. Should I live to the next centennial, I shall never forget that moment.

The girl who had spoken last stooped and looked under the bed; this motion was followed by a thrilling shriek.

"There's a *man* under the bed!" she screamed.

The other girls joined in; a wild chorus of shrieks arose, commingled with cries of "Robber!" "Thief!" "Burglar!"

Urged to desperation, I was about to roll out from my hiding-place and make a rush to get out, hoping to pass unrecognized by covering my face with my hands, when two or three dozen young men swooped into the room.

"What is it?"

"Where?"

"A man under the bed!"

"Let me at the rascal!"

"Ha! come out here, you villain!"

All was over. They dragged me out, covered with dust and feathers, and, pulling my despairing hands from over my miserable face, they turned me to the light. Then the fury and the threats subsided. There was a moment's profound silence—girls and fellows stared in mute astonishment, and then—then broke from one and all a burst of convulsive laughter. And in the midst of those shrieks and groans of mirth at my expense, everything grew dark, and I suffered no more. They told me afterward that I fainted dead away.

CHAPTER XVIII.

HE OPENS THE WRONG DOOR.

My mother and the ancient lady who presided over the mysteries of my initiation as a member of the human fraternity, say that I was born with a caul over my face. Now, what I want to know is, why didn't they leave that caul where they found it? What business had they to meddle with the veil which beneficent nature gave me as a shield to my infirmity? Had they respected her intention, they would have let it alone—poked a hole in it for me to eat and breathe through, and left the veil which she kindly provided to hide my blushing face from the eyes of my fellow-creatures.

Nature knew beforehand that I was going to be born to be bashful. Therefore she gave me a caul. Had this been respected as it should have been, I could have blossomed out into my full luxuriance as a *cauli*flower whereas now I am an ever-blooming peony.

When I rushed home after recovering from the fainting fit into which my hiding under the bed had driven me, I threw myself down in he sanctity of my private apartment and howled and shrieked for that caul of my infancy. But no caul came at my call. That dried and withered thing was reposing somewhere amid the curiosities of an old hag's bureau-drawer.

Then I wildly wished that I were the veiled prophet of Khorassan. But no! I was only bashful John Flutter, the butt and ridicule of a little meddling village.

I knew that this last adventure would revive the memory of all my previous exploits. I knew the girls would all go to see each other the next day so as to have a good giggle together. Worse than that, I knew there would be an unprecedented run of custom at the store. There wouldn't be a girl in the whole place who wouldn't require something in the dry-goods line the coming day; they would come and ask for pins and needles just for the heartless fun of seeing *me* enduring the pangs of mental pins and needles.

So I resolved that I would not get up that morning. The breakfast-bell rang three times; mother came up to knock at my door.

"Oh, I am so sleepy, mother!" I answered, with a big yawn; "you knew I was up last night. Don't want any breakfast, just another little nap."

So the good soul went down, leaving me to my wretched thoughts. At noon she came up again.

"John, you had better rise now. Father can't come to dinner there's so many customers in the store. Seems as if there was going to be a ball to-night again; every girl in town is after ribbon, or lace, or hair-pins, or something."

"I can't get up to-day, mother. I'm awfully unwell—got a high fever—*you'll* have to go in and lend father a helping hand"; and so she brought me a cup of tea and a piece of toast, and then went up to take father's place while he ate his dinner.

I *guess* she suspected I'd been done for again by the way those young women laughed when she told them I was sick in bed: for she was pretty cross when I sneaked down to tea, and didn't seem to worry about how I felt. Well, I kept pretty quiet the rest of the season. There were dances and sleighing parties, but I stayed away from them, and attended strictly to business.

I don't know but that I might have begun to enjoy some peace of mind, after the winter and part of the spring had passed without any very awful catastrophe having occurred to me; but, some time in the latter part of May, when the roses were just beginning to bloom, and everything was lovely, a pretty cousin from some distant part of the State came to spend a month at our house. I had never seen her before, and you may imagine how I felt when she rushed at me and kissed me, and called me her dear cousin John, just as if we had known each other all the days of our lives. I think it was a constant surprise to her to find that I was bashful. *She* wasn't a bit so. It embarrassed me a thousand times more to see how she would slyly watch out of the corner of her laughing eye for the signs of my diffidence.

Well, of course, all the girls called on her, and boys too, as to that, and I had to take her to return their visits, and I was in hot water all the time. Before she went away, mother gave her a large evening party. I behaved with my usual elegance of manner, stepping on the ladies' trains and toes in dancing, calling them by other people's names, and all those little courtesies for which I was so famous. I even contrived to sit down where there was no chair, to the amusement of the fellows. My cousin Susie was going away the next day. I was dead in love with her, and my mind was taken up with the intention of telling her so. I had not the faintest idea of whether she cared for me or not. She had laughed at me and teased me mercilessly.

On the contrary, she had been very encouraging to Tom Todd, a young lawyer of the place—a little snob, with self-conceit enough in his dapper body for six larger men. This evening he had been particularly attentive to her. Susie was pretty and quite an heiress, so I knew Tom Todd would try to secure her. He was just that kind of a fellow who could propose to a girl while he was asking her out for a set of the lanciers, or handing her a plate of salad at supper. Alas, I could do nothing of the kind. With all my superior opportunities, here the last evening was half through, and I had not yet made a motion to secure the prize. I watched Tom as if he had been a thief and I a detective. I was cold and hot by turns whenever he bent to whisper in Susie's ear, as he did about a thousand times. At last, as supper-time approached, I saw my cousin slip out into the dining-room. I thought mother had sent her to see that all was right, before marshalling the company out to the feast.

"Now, or never," I thought, turning pale as death; and with one resolute effort I slipped into the hall and so into the dining-room.

Susie was there, doing something; but when she saw me enter she gave a little shriek and darted into the pantry. No! I was not to be baffled thus. A cold sweat broke out on my forehead, but I thought of that snob in the parlor, and pressed on to the pantry-door.

"Susie," said I, very softly, trying to open it—"Susie, I *must* speak to you. Let me in."

The more I tried to open the door the more firmly she held it.

"Do go along with you, cousin John," she answered.

"I can't, Susie. I want to see you a minute."

"See me? Oh, what a wicked fellow! Go along, or I'll tell your mother."

"Tell, or not; for once I'm going to have my own way," I said, and pressing my knee against the door, I forced it open, and there stood my pretty cousin, angry and blushing, trying to hide from my view the crinoline which had come off in the parlor.

I retreated, closing the door and waiting for her to re-appear.

In a few minutes she came out, evidently offended.

"Susie," I stammered, "I did—did—didn't dream your bus—bus—bustle had come off. I only wanted to tell you that—that I pr—pr—pri—prize your li—li—li—"

"But I never lie," she interrupted me, saucily.

"That I shall be the most mis—is—is—er—able fellow that ever—"

"Now don't make a goose of yourself, cousin John," she said, sweetly, laying her little hand on my shoulder for an instant. "Stop where you are! Tom Todd asked me to marry him, half an hour ago, and I said I would."

Tom Todd, then, had got the start of me; after all. Worse! he had sneaked into the dining-room after Susie, and had come up behind us and heard every word. As I turned, dizzy and confused, I saw his smiling, insolent face. Enraged, unhappy, and embarrassed by his grieving triumph, I hastily turned to retreat into the pantry! Unfortunately, there were two doors close together, one leading to the pantry, the other to the cellar. In my blind embarrassment I mistook them; and the next moment the whole company were startled by a loud bump—bumping, a crash, and a woman's scream.

There was a barrel of soft-soap at the foot of the cellar-stairs, and I fell, head first, into that.

CHAPTER XIX.

DRIVEN FROM HIS LAST DEFENCE.

Susie was Mrs. Todd before I recovered from the effects of my involuntary soap-bath.

"Smart trick!" cried my father when he fished me out of the barrel.

I thought it *was* smart, sure enough, by the sensation in my eyes. But I have drawn a veil over that bit of my history. I know my eyesight was injured for all that summer. I could not tell a piece of silk from a piece of calico, except by the feeling; so I was excused from clerking in the store, and sat round the house with green goggles on, and wished I were different from what I was. By fall my eyesight got better. One day father came in the parlor where I was sitting moping, having just seen Tom Todd drive by in a new buggy with his bride, and said to me:

"John, I am disappointed in you."

"I know it," I answered him meekly.

"You look well enough, and you have talent enough," he went on; "but you are too ridiculously bashful for an ostrich."

"I know it," I again replied. "Oh, father, father, why did they take that caul from my face?"

"That—what?" inquired my puzzled sire.

"That caul—wasn't I born with a caul, father?"

"Now that I recall it, I believe you were," responded father, while his stern face relaxed into a smile, "and I wish to goodness they had left it on you, John; but they didn't, and that's an end of it. What I was going to say was this. Convinced that you will never succeed as my successor—that your unconquerable diffidence unfits you for the dry-goods trade—I have been looking around for some such situation as I have often heard you sigh for. The old light-house keeper on Buncombe Island is dead, and I have caused you to be appointed his successor. You will not see a human being except when supplies are brought to you, which, in the winter, will be only once in two months. Even then your peace will not be disturbed by any sight of one of the other sex. You will not need a caul there! Go, my son, and remain until you can outgrow your absurd infirmity."

I felt dismayed at the prospect, now that it was so near at hand. I had often—in the distance—yearned for the security of a light-house. Yet I now looked about on our comfortable parlor with a longing eye. I recalled the pleasant tea-hour when there were no visitors; I thought of the fun the boys and girls would have this coming winter, and I wished father had not been so precipitate in securing that vacant place.

Just then Miss Gabble came up our steps, and shortly after entered the parlor. She was one of those dreaded beings, who always filled me with the direst confusion. She sat right down by my side and squeezed my hand.

"My poor, dear fellow-mortal!" said she, getting her sharp face so close to mine I thought she was going to kiss me, "how do you do? Wearing them goggles yet? It is too bad. And yet, after all, they are sort of becoming to you. In fact, you're so good-looking you can wear anything. And how your mustache does grow, to be sure!"

I saw father was getting up to leave the room, and I flung her hand away, saying quickly to him: "I'll get the glass of water, father."

And so I beat him that time, and got out of the room, quite willing to live in the desert of Sahara, if by it I could get rid of such females.

Well, I went to Buncombe Island. I retired from the world to a light-house in the first bloom of my youth. I did not want to be a monk—I could not be a man—and so I did what fate and my father laid out for me to do. Through the fine autumn weather I enjoyed my retirement. I had taken plenty of books and magazines with me to while away the time; there was a lovely promenade along the sea-wall on which the tall tower stood, and I could walk there for hours without my pulse being disturbed by visions of parasols, loves of bonnets, and pretty faces under them. I communed with the sea. I told it my rations were too salt; that I didn't like the odor of the oil in filling the lamps; that my legs got tired going up to the lantern, and that my arms gave out polishing the lenses. I also confided to it that I would not mind these little trifles if I only had one being to share my solitude—a modest, shy little creature that I wouldn't be afraid to ask to be my wife.

> "Oh, had we some bright little isle of our own,
> In a blue summer ocean far off and alone."

I'd forget the curse of my life and be happy in spite of it.

When winter shut down, however, I didn't talk quite so much to the sea; it was ugly and boisterous, and the windy promenade was dangerous, and I shut myself up and pined like the "Prisoner of Chillon." I have lots of spunk and pride, if I am bashful; and so I never let on to those at home—when I sent them a letter once in two months by the little tug that brought my oil and provisions—that I was homesick. I said the ocean was glorious; that there was a Byronic sublimity in lighting up the lantern; that standing behind a counter and showing dry-goods to silly, giggling girls couldn't be compared with it; that I hadn't blushed in six months, and that I didn't think I should ever be willing to come back to a world full of grinning snobs and confusing women.

And now, what do you think happened to me? My fate was too strong even for Buncombe Island. It was the second of January. The tug had not left the island, after leaving a nine-weeks' supply, more than twelve hours before a fearful gale began to blow; it rose higher and higher through the night, and in the morning I found that a small sailing-vessel had been wrecked about half a mile from the light-house, where the beach ran out for some distance into the water, and the land was not so high as on the rock. I ran down there, the wind still roaring enough to blow me away, and the spray dashing into my eyes, and I found the vessel had gone to pieces and every man was drowned.

But what was this that lay at my feet? A woman, lashed to a spar, and apparently dead. When I picked her up, though, she opened her eyes and shut them again. Enough! this was no time to think of peculiar difficulties. I lugged her to the warm room in the light-house where I sat and lived. I put her before the fire; I heated some brandy and poured it between her lips; in short, when I sat down to my little tea-table late that afternoon, somebody sat on the opposite side—a woman—a girl, rather, not more than eighteen or nineteen. Here she was, and here she must remain for two long months.

She did not seem half so much put out as I. In fact, she was quite calm, after she had explained to me that she was one of three passengers on board the sailing-vessel, and that all the others were drowned.

"You will have to remain here for two months," I ventured to explain to her, coloring like a lobster dabbed into hot water.

"Oh, then, I may as well begin pouring the tea at once," she observed coolly; "that's a feminine duty, you know, sir."

"I'm glad you're not afraid of me," I ventured to say.

"Afraid of you!" she replied, tittering. "No, indeed. It is *you* who are afraid of *me*. But I sha'n't hurt you, sir. You mind your affairs, and I'll mind mine, and neither of us will come to grief. Why, what a lot of books you've got! And such an easy-chair! It's just splendid here, and so romantic, like the stories we read."

I repressed a groan, and allowed her, after supper, and she had done as she said—washed the dishes—to take possession of my favorite book and my favorite seat. She was tired with her adventures of the night before, and soon asked where she was to sleep.

"In there," I answered, pointing to the door of a small bedroom which opened out of the living-room.

She went in, and locked the door; and I went up to the lantern to see that all was right, and to swear and tear around a little. Here was a two-months'-long embarrassment! Here was all my old trouble back in a new shape! What would my folks—what would the world say?

Would they believe the story about the wreck? Must my character suffer? Even at the best, I must face this girl of the period from morning until night. She had already discovered that I was bashful; she would take advantage of it to torment me. What would the rude men say when they came again with supplies?

Better measure tape in my father's store for a lot of teasing young ladies whom I know, than dwell alone in a light-house with this inconsiderate young woman!

"If ever I get out of this scrape, I will know when I am well off!" I moaned, tearing my hair, and gazing wildly at the pitiless lights.

Suddenly a thought struck me. I had seen a small boat beached near the scene of the wreck; it probably had belonged to the ship. I remained in the lantern until it began to grow daybreak; then I crept down and out, and ran to examine that boat. It was water-proof, and one of its oars still remained. The waves were by this time comparatively calm. I pushed the boat into the water, jumped in, rowed around to the other side of the island, and that day I made thirty miles, with only one oar, landing at the city dock at sunset. I was pretty well used-up I tell you. But I had got away from that solitary female, who must have spent a pensive day at Buncombe, in wondering what had become of me. I reported at headquarters that night, resigned, and started for home. I'm afraid the light-house lamps were not properly tended that night; still, they may have been, and that girl was equal to anything.

Such is life! Such has been *my* experience. Do you wonder that I am still a bachelor? I will not go on, relating circumstances in my life which have too much resemblance to each other. It would only be a repetition of my miserable blunders. But I will make a proposition to young ladies in general. I am well-to-do; the store is in a most flourishing condition; I have but one serious fault, and you all know what that is. Now, will not some of you take pity on me? I might be waylaid, blindfolded, lifted into a carriage, and abducted. I might be brought before a minister and frightened into marrying any nice, handsome, well-bred girl that had courage enough for such an emergency. Once safely wedded, I have a faint idea that my bashfulness will wear off. Come! who is ready to try the experiment?